Other Books by Carol Shackleford

THE WINDOW TRILOGY

The Underwater Window

The Discovered Windows

The Broken Window

Happy reading!

Carol Shackleford

ADA GRACE

By Carol Shackleford

Chapter 1

All she could hear was the sound of the wall clock ticking and her own deep breaths as her heart pounded in fear. Standing in the arched doorway between the kitchen and living room, she stared at the curtains covering the front window. She had been talking herself into this moment for weeks. Today was two years since her dear Charley had left her alone. There was no stopping the memories from flooding back just like they did every time she looked toward the window. It was two years ago when she was looking out that window watching for him to return from a short walk down to the corner. It felt like yesterday and it felt like a lifetime ago.

Charley was trying to get in his small bit of exercise on this last day of September. Soon it would be too cold to enjoy any outside activity. Once the snow arrived, it wasn't worth the risk of slipping and falling on ice.

Ada usually went with him but today she had awakened with a sore throat and cough. Being certain that it was just her fall allergies, she brushed off the idea of going to the doctor. But when it came time for their daily walk, Charley had insisted that she stay in and rest. She didn't like him to go alone so she tried to protest. He was very convincing with his argument, "Ada Grace, if it is indeed allergies, then being outside would be the worst thing for ya."

The breeze was rustling the leaves on the tree between the house and sidewalk. She was sitting in the chair looking out at the tidy little row of houses that lined their street. They had watched neighbors come and go over the years. It was an old neighborhood with tiny houses. Nowadays, they agreed, everyone wanted big houses with big yards and big garages. And a big mortgage, they would always say and chuckle together. Charley and Ada had lived in this comfortable two-bedroom home for 62 years. Sure, they had made improvements as were needed but much of it had stayed the same which was just how they both wanted it.

Twisting her left wrist to once again look at her watch, she decided it was taking too long for Charley's walk. She decided to go put on her shoes and walk out to meet him. He had been slowing down more lately. Usually, he just stopped to catch his breath and after a minute or two would continue on. He probably just started visiting with a neighbor, she thought, trying to reassure herself. Scooting herself forward towards the edge of the chair to stand up, she started coughing. As her coughing subsided long enough for her to push herself up out of the chair, her body froze as she noticed a police car stop in front of the house. She quickly made her way to the door as the officer walked up the sidewalk.

The young officer looked at her with kind, sad eyes. She swallowed and held her breath as she waited for him to speak. "Ma'am, are you Charles Eldon's wife?"

Realizing her voice wouldn't work, she just nodded her head.

Looking at the ground for a long second before looking back into her eyes, he quietly stated, "I'm sorry to inform you that your husband has passed away. Someone driving by saw him walking on the sidewalk then he just fell over. When they got out of their vehicle to check on him, he wasn't breathing. They called an ambulance right away but he was already gone when they got there. Is there anybody I can call for you?" he asked with sympathy.

Ada heard what the officer told her but her mind wasn't allowing her to process it. She felt as if she wasn't part of the conversation. She stared at him but he could tell she was not seeing him. He gently led her by her elbow to sit in the chair she had just gotten up from. "Ma'am, I'm going to go in the kitchen to get you a glass of water, is that ok?" With no response from her, he quietly left the room to find the cabinet with glasses. After filling it up with tap water, he came back and knelt down on one knee next to her chair. She didn't acknowledge the glass so the officer spoke quietly, "Mrs. Eldon?" After a few times of speaking her name, she slowly turned her head to look at him. He motioned to the glass of water as he handed it to her. She blinked and reached for the glass. She started looking around the room and swallowed hard as her gaze landed on the police car outside the window.

Looking back to the officer, she shook her head and handed the glass of water back to him. "Charley!" She hollered in a frightened, hoarse voice.

"Ma'am, is there anyone I can call for you?" asked the officer calmly.

"No. I need to get Charley. I should have gone with him. He shouldn't be walking alone." Ada started coughing and the officer tried to calm her down.

"Mrs. Eldon, is there a neighbor I could get to come over for a while?"

"No. Take me to Charley." Her hands were trembling and her face was draining of color. "Charley!" She called out as big tears welled in the corners of her eyes and one by one starting sliding down the side of her pale cheeks.

The officer reached for his radio to call for an ambulance feeling like she was probably going into shock. As he was about to radio in, the front door opened and a large man stood in the doorway blocking most of the light from coming through. He made eye contact with Ada and rushed over to her side. Bending down he enveloped her in a giant hug.

"Aunt A, I'm here." Ada melted into him and started sobbing until it caught in her throat and she started coughing. Looking up at the officer, they nodded a greeting to each other. The officer said with some relief in his voice, "Joe, it's good to see you. I was about to call in a medical." He handed the glass of water to Joe. With some coaxing and a soothing voice, Joe got Ada to get some sips of water down. He reached up to feel her forehead for a fever and took her frail wrist in his oversized hand to get her pulse. Glancing up at the officer, Joe nodded his head to call in for an ambulance. While the ambulance was being arranged, Joe talked to Ada.

"Aunt A, I'm here. Look at me, can you?" Joe twisted down so he could look into her eyes. They were glassy and not focusing on him. "Aunt A. Come on. Look at me."

Ada looked at the ground. "Charley. My Charley. He went out to walk. Go help him." Her voice was barely above a whisper. "Joey. Please. Go help him."

Chapter 2

Ada didn't remember much after that for several weeks. Her battle with the flu had kept her in the hospital for several days. Joe had been worried about how much of her illness had been heartache that she would never recover from. Eventually she was well enough to have Charley's funeral. Thankfully Charley and Ada had long since made all the arrangements knowing it would be too stressful for either of them to think it all through right after the loss. Ada had always told him, "Charley, you know I will have to go first. I couldn't live without you."

He would smile, wink at her and slowly shake his head. "Ada Grace, you would be ok. You are the strongest gal I know."

She would tease him with her reply, "Oh really? And how many gals do you know?"

"I know lots of gals but you are the only one I have eyes for. My heart beats for you alone." He would say as he wiggled his eyebrows up and down and patted his chest with his open hand.

It always got the desired response. A slight blush, a huge smile that almost made her eyes disappear and a soft sigh of pure contentment.

Their love had started instantly and grown intensely over the years. It all started 63 years prior when Ada had been a week away from her eighteenth birthday. It was a clear, cloudless day with a damp chill in the air which most certainly indicated fall was here and winter was sure to be coming shortly. Ada had been struggling with a heavy load she had just purchased from the general store. As she was walking the short distance back to her parent's home, she dropped first one item then another. From behind her, she heard a friendly voice ask, "Can I help you with that?" She stood up and looked into the eyes of the young man who instantly stole her heart.

Her eyes quickly pulled away from his smiling gaze as she looked down at her feet. Before she was able to answer, two more items dropped from her bag, hitting the ground with a thud and just barely missing her foot. Charley chuckled as he reached for her bag with a few of the remaining items still looking as if they may fall out at any time. "I guess that's my answer."

Ada couldn't help but laugh. He could have made her feel stupid for not bringing along two bags. She never was very good at calculating volume. "I guess you better before I damage everything." She quickly reached down to pick up the fallen goods.

After that first encounter, they had seen each other every day. Each day learning more about one another. Their pasts, hopes, fears and future plans. There had never been a question that any plans for the future would be spent together. They got married a few months later on Christmas Eve and on each anniversary, they continued what they called Their Anniversary Tradition.

All of these memories were running through Ada's mind as she looked at the curtains. Heavy and dark. They did a good job of keeping out the light. The thick window dressings even seemed to keep out a bit of neighborhood noise and some of the chill from cold nights. As she looked at them, she realized that for the past two years, they were also keeping out the full reality that her life had changed permanently. The fear of opening them and knowing she would never look out to a life with her best friend and companion being at her side almost took her breath away. But after two years, she knew it was time. Charley would want her to continue to live. She didn't want to. In her mind, she was not the strong gal he thought she was. Sure, she was strong when he was around. He built her up and made her feel like she could conquer the world. But without him at her side, she didn't know how to live.

Ada could still remember sitting in her chair for weeks after the funeral, just staring at the curtains. How many times had she wished she could pull the draw cord to open the bulky divide between herself and the outside and have it all be just a bad dream. She would be relieved to wake from the awful nightmare. But she knew if she pulled that cord to open up to a new day, it would be a day without Charley. She didn't want that day. If she kept them closed, she could live in denial and keep the faint hope of a nightmare alive. But with each passing day, she felt the burden of the darkness weighing down not only her spirit but her memories. It was time to let the light shine in to both, but she didn't know if she was truly strong enough.

Feeling shaky and weak, she slowly put one foot in front of the other. With heart pounding, ears buzzing, and tears streaming down her face, she reached for the cord to open the curtains. With her hand grasping the cord with unnecessary tightness, she said out loud to herself, "Ok, Charley. Here we go. It's time to live again."

Ada pulled the cord slowly down and the curtains began separating in the middle letting the sunlight glance through the small opening. As she continued pulling, the draperies each traveled their own way toward an opposite wall. Dust particles danced in the sunlight as the bright light made its first appearance in over 700 days. She wanted to stop and reverse course. Close them up again. Shutting her eyes tight to block out the light and the memories of that police car which were already starting to come back, she gave one last good tug and felt the tension of the cord that indicated the completion of her task.

Taking a deep breath, Ada willed herself to open her scrunched up eyelids. It was so bright, she almost had to close her eyes again. She squinted at the rays of dancing light coming through the window. It crossed her mind that the sun is out every day. Even in the midst of severe storms, it's up there waiting for the storm to pass and the clouds to part. Even if you can't see it, it's still there. One hundred percent dependable. Sometimes we go through periods when we choose not to see or acknowledge it. Ada had chosen to ignore the sun for exactly two years.

She took the necessary steps to walk over to the chair which had been designated from the very beginning as hers. Hers was on the left, Charley's on the right. They had tried once to sit in each other's chair and it felt just plain strange. She looked from his chair to hers. They were identical in every way other than the spots where they were worn. Funny how she never noticed that before. They must have sat differently and used different parts of the arm rests to help them get out of the chair. Ada smiled sadly as she remembered them teasing each other when they noticed they had to grunt a little to get up. It really did help. They had agreed on that one hundred percent.

Ada took her seat on the left. She reached over and stroked the arm of the chair on the right. Letting out a deep sigh, she leaned back and took her first glimpse out the window. She noticed right away that it was dirty. Feeling slightly embarrassed for letting it get so bad, she put it on her mental list to clean it right away. Normally she didn't put much faith in her mental notes. If she wanted to remember something, she had to write it down. But Ada had a feeling she wouldn't need to write it down since it was a reminder each time she looked out. Her eyes started a slow scan of the neighborhood. Joe had kept her updated about the events in the area. He let her know which homes were for sale or if someone was sick. He informed her when someone had a new baby or grand baby. I guess that's the benefit of small-town living. Most people knew each other.

After Charley's funeral, many of the neighbors had brought over food and given huge doses of sympathy and condolences. Everyone knew Charley.

17

And to know him was to love him. His kind nature. His unusual and contagious laugh. He would help anyone with anything at any time. Ada had appreciated all of the thoughtful gestures but after a while people just go back to living their lives. Their lives hadn't changed and she didn't blame them one bit. Plus, she knew she had not been very neighborly at that time. She had not wanted to visit or offer coffee or tea. Everyone loved her tea. Hot or iced, hers was the best around. That's what they all said anyway. She wanted to be alone. In the dark. With her thoughts and memories. Sure, she supposed some people wanted to share stories and talk about the recent loss but not her. Sometimes she would pretend it hadn't happened and that when she woke up in the morning it would all have been a bad nightmare. But each morning, much to her despair, it was not a nightmare. It was her new life. And she hated it.

Something caught Ada's eye out the window. She glanced up just in time to see a squirrel run up the tree followed closely by another squirrel. Around and around the base of the tree they went. Out on this limb than that one. They looked to her like a cartoon. She couldn't help but smile a little. As quick as they arrived, they departed. Flying across the street in an apparent race to see which one could get there first.

It was at that moment that she noticed the boy. He was standing on the sidewalk across the street. He was small and looked too young to be out there alone. She glanced around but didn't see anyone else. Making eye contact with him, she studied his face. Her eyesight had always been pretty good. Even as she aged and required glasses, she was grateful to have such good vision. He looked to be about 4 or 5 years old. His eyes looked drawn like they were tired. He nervously peeked around behind him to the front door of the house he was standing in front of. Turning back to look at Ada, he cocked his head slightly, a slight smile crossed his face and he cautiously raised his hand in a wave. Feeling her heart melt, she smiled and waved back. Suddenly, he jumped like he had been startled. With a panicked look on his innocent face, he turned and quickly ran around the side of the house he had been standing in front of. About ten seconds later, a blue pick-up truck with a gray door and a shattered passenger side windshield came to a screeching halt in front of the house. An angry looking younger man jumped out of the driver's side door and slammed it shut behind him. He started heading to the front door then stopped in his tracks and spun around. He looked at her through the window and scowled. Turning back around, he stormed up to the house and pushed the door in with such force, Ada would have been surprised if it didn't break the door.

For the rest of the day, Ada worried about that little boy. As she went to bed that night, she wondered if by opening the curtains, she had opened a can of worms she didn't want to get in the middle of.

Chapter 3

After a fitful night's sleep, Ada was more than ready to start her day and noticed that her heart didn't pound nearly as much as she made her way to open the curtains. Maybe soon she would do it without even thinking about it. She wasn't feeling very hopeful about it. But it could happen, she thought without much optimism. Standing in front of the large window, she surveyed the neighborhood. It looked pretty quiet and very peaceful. It was still too early for the bus to come by to pick up the kids at the bus stop on the corner. A car drove by and came to an abrupt halt just past the house. Ada recognized the car as belonging to the middle-aged man named Bruce from three doors down. Putting the car in reverse, he backed up and rolled down the window. Leaning out he waved in exaggerated form and gave a thumbs up. He was smiling so big she couldn't help but smile and wave back.

Wandering into the kitchen, she began her usual morning routine. One egg, over easy with a piece of buttered toast and a glass of orange juice with her morning pills. It never occurred to either Charley or Ada to shake up their breakfast ritual. They used to eat a hearty breakfast every morning before Charley left for work. But one day shortly after retirement, while trying to decide between bacon and sausage, Charley had thought about it and said, "You know, I don't much care for decisions so early of a mornin. How about just eggs and toast. Can't go wrong with just eggs and toast. What do ya say, Ada Grace?" And just eggs and toast it was from that day forward.

She looked into her hand at the couple of pills and wondered what they were for. Their nephew, Joe, was the town doctor and for about the past ten years, he had made sure to have Charley and Ada's pills all ready for them each week. When Charley started having heart trouble, it became difficult to figure out all of the medicines and which ones to take how often, so they were more than happy to accept his offer of help.

Charley used to get the newspaper every morning and sit in his chair to read it from cover to cover. If he came to an interesting story he thought she would enjoy, he would read it out loud as she sat to his left crocheting tiny hats and sweaters for the church. She didn't remember where her creations ended up but she didn't care. She just enjoyed keeping her hands busy with an activity that could benefit an infant wherever it was needed. After hearing the daily weather prediction and the scores of local sports teams, she would offer up answers or guesses to the crossword puzzle clues. They always got a kick out of knowing answers because they remembered them from prior puzzles. Charley always said, "How'd we get so smart, Ada Grace?" After the funeral, Joe eventually cancelled the newspaper since Ada wouldn't bring them into the house. They accumulated on the porch and Joe would gather them up each week during his visit only to be told to leave them outside.

Shaking her head to clear away the sadness that was starting to invade her morning, she got up from the table to wash the plate, glass, fork and knife. Just as she closed the silverware drawer after placing the clean utensils to their proper places, Ada heard a strange noise coming from the living room. Peeking her head through the arched door opening, she almost jumped out of her skin when she saw someone standing right in front of the window. It took only a moment to recognize the face staring in at her. It was her dear friend and next-door neighbor, Cynthia. She was standing on the second step of a stool and had window cleaner and paper towels on the top step. She had started at the top and was working her way down. Cynthia's face lit up when she saw Ada walk into the room. Ada walked over to the window and through the glass said loudly, "Thank you!"

Cynthia nodded her head. She had been shocked when she went out for her morning walk and saw that Ada's curtains had been opened. For almost a year, Cynthia had tried to visit with Ada following her husband's funeral. Ada wouldn't let anyone other than Joe into the house and she hadn't left the house in two years. After a year of trying, Cynthia decided to give her the space she requested but still brought over fresh baked cookies every Monday afternoon and left them on the little table outside the front door. She sent her little notes in the mail just to keep in touch. Feeling overjoyed to see her friend beginning to open up again, she had to hold back her enthusiasm knowing that Ada would let her know when she was ready to communicate in person again. She spoke through the glass back to her friend, "Oatmeal with chocolate chips this afternoon."

Ada grinned. Cynthia knew that was her favorite cookie. Well, at least she knew it was a Monday now. About the only way she had to judge the days any more were Monday cookies and Joe's Wednesday night and Sunday afternoon visits.

Feeling energetic for the first time in a long time, Ada decided to do some laundry. She began the task of removing the sheets from the bed. If she had known she was going to wash them today, she wouldn't have made the bed this morning. She chuckled to herself at the thought. It almost startled her to hear the sound come out. It had been entirely too long since she chuckled to herself.

After starting the washing machine, Ada decided that since the window was so clean now, she better get out the dust rag because the sunlight really showed how long she had ignored this dreaded chore. Of all the work around the house that needed to be done, dusting had always been her least favorite. Maybe that was why it always felt so rewarding once the task was complete. Before she started, she walked over to the little clock radio on top of the bread box. Pushing the power button, quiet music started floating through the house. She clicked the volume button up two notches and by the time she put the dust rag to furniture, she was humming.

Chapter 4

As a new morning dawned, Ada found herself looking forward to getting up and opening her curtains. Today the window revealed an overcast sky that looked like it could drop a storm at any minute. Tree branches were bending in the strong wind and leaves were coming off trees, blowing through the air like giant confetti. It looked like the weather forecast was correct on the news last night. She hoped they wouldn't get the hail that had been mentioned. Sitting down in her chair to think about what she could do that day, she tried not to obsess about the house across the street. She couldn't get that little boy's face out of her mind. She hadn't seen any activity over there since the incident the other day. Wondering if he was afraid of storms, she worried about him being alone and scared.

The sight of an all-white cat peeking through the glass distracted her attention away from her worries. "Well, hello there," Ada said aloud as she got up to take a closer look. The cat had jumped onto one of the two creaky old outdoor rockers on the front porch. His front paws stretched up the back of the chair so he was able to get a good view inside. "Aren't you a darling little thing. Where did you come from?" She didn't remember the cat from before. It could be a neighbor's cat. Or maybe someone just dumped it there. Several of the neighbors had complained of that in the past. People just decided they didn't want an animal any longer and would drop it off hoping someone else would take care of it. That seemed like a dirty thing to do in her opinion. Before she could think about what might be available in her cupboard to feed it, he jumped down from the chair and took off like a rocket. Just seconds later, rolling rumbles of thunder started up followed instantly by lightning. The dark sky lit up as the storm began. Headlights broke through the stormy darkness and Ada was still standing next to the window when Bruce slowly rolled by giving a short beep of his horn and waving from inside the vehicle. She waved back enthusiastically, hoping he would safely get to his job in the bad weather.

Feeling more enthusiastic than she had felt in too long, she got the little yellow pad of paper out of the drawer by the refrigerator. It was high time she made a list. She used to love lists. There had been no need for them after Charley wasn't around. Lists were for ideas and projects. Things to do today and this week and maybe it even involved a whole month if it was something she didn't really want to do because then it went to the bottom of the page. Some lists had those darn items that never seemed to get crossed off. Lists always provided just a bit of control. Control over what was chosen to tackle on the list. But with Charley gone, what was the point? There had been nothing to put on the list. What did it matter if the linen closet got re-organized or the seasonal clothes were brought to the front of their small closet? Nothing mattered. There was no control over anything. She had lost everything.

But today, with a whole lot more optimism than she thought she could muster, she put pen to paper. Plenty of things needed to be done. First on the list was 'make a grocery list'. She smiled to herself when she thought of Charley teasing her about her lists of lists. He would often add something to the bottom of the list. 'Give your husband a smooch'. or 'Look in the mirror and wink at yourself.' And Ada would do it with a grin and then happily go cross it off her list. While she was thinking about what else to add to what would certainly be a long list of to-do's, she was also thinking about what to put on her grocery list. She was going to surprise Joey and make him his favorite meal. Of course, it wouldn't be too much of a surprise since he brought over her groceries every week. In the middle of her thinking about mozzarella cheese and dusting off the top of the refrigerator, she heard a commotion outside. She slowly got up from the kitchen table and went to the living room to look out.

It was still dark and gloomy but the rain had slowed to just a drizzle. Looking over at the clock, she was surprised to see it was already almost time for the school bus to arrive. Some of the kids were hollering to each other as they ran down the sidewalk intentionally trying to hit every puddle on the way.

They all gathered on the corner across the street. Jeannie lived on that corner and had two children of her own. Ada had always been amazed on days when it was extra cold and snowy or damp and rainy or maybe just because one of the children was wanting a friendly face, Jeannie would open her door and let all of the children gather in her house waiting for the bus to arrive. Ada was quite certain she would never be able to do that. So much snow and muddy feet and commotion. Surely it took Jeannie an hour each morning to clean up the outcome of all those shoes and boots. Looking down the street as the stop sign popped out from the side of the bus and about a dozen loud, lively kids boarded, Ada felt certain that none of those children appreciated what Jeannie did for them. But she also felt certain that someday they would. Ada hoped that maybe just a few of them might tell her thank you.

About to head back into the kitchen, a movement caught her eye. She watched as the pretty white cat climbed back up on her porch chair. He stared at her through the window. Ada surprised herself when a happy sound escaped her throat. If she didn't know better, she might think that it was another chuckle. Tipping her head to one side she tried to think of what she had in the kitchen to feed this little guy. Not used to using her voice, she quietly said, "Well, fella, if you are going to stay for a minute, I will see what I can find." As if he understood her, he turned his back and sat on the chair watching the street for any activity and seemed patient to wait for his breakfast.

After chopping up the small piece of left-over chicken from the night before, Ada placed it in an old cool whip container and headed to the front door. She only had a reason to open the door when Cynthia left a meal or cookies. She hesitated for a second. Looking over to the rocking chair, she didn't see the cat. Feeling disappointed, she cracked open the door and peeked out the small opening. Sitting facing the door like he owned the place, was her breakfast guest. He took a step toward the door as if waiting for her to open the screen door and permit him to enter. She spoke right to him, "No way. You are not coming in here." She leaned over and slowly opened the screen door just enough to allow the cool whip container to squeeze through the opening. Looking just a little disgusted at her refusal for admittance, one whiff of the chicken had his attention. With tail swishing and ears twitching and perking up at any little noise, he ate quickly and defensively. Watching him chow down his food, she was pleased when he quickly finished but then proceeded to sit and stare at her while licking his chops for several minutes. Ada assumed it was to get all the last little chicken bits from his whiskers. "Well, if you are going to be around once in a while, I suppose I better give you a name. Now, if you already have a name, this will just be your nickname." She stared into her thought space for just a few seconds before announcing, "I will call you Oliver. I've always liked that name. Do you think Oliver will work?" He plopped down with a thud and rolled to his back as if expecting her to pet him. With a slight grin, she leaned down slightly and said, "Well, now you are just expecting too much." Standing up, she turned to shut the door, locking it behind her like she always did.

As she sat down at the table to continue her list making, the phone rang. She didn't care who it was. She wasn't up to talking to anyone. After several rings, the answering machine picked up and she could hear Charley's voice. "Sorry we missed your call. If you leave a message, we will call you back. Unless you are selling something." Following the beep was a message from the pastor from Charley and Ada's church. Ada had to give him credit for not giving up on her. He called every week and left a message. If she was completely honest with herself, her appreciation wasn't necessarily because of what his message said but because every time he called, she got to hear Charley's voice on the machine. It also tended to leave her a bit melancholy for the rest of the day. Although the sun was now showing itself after the morning storms, her demeanor was now heading in the wrong direction. Ada started pacing the floor with one hand wringing the other. Taking turns squeezing her fingers in a tight grip switching from hand to hand. When she finally acknowledged what she was doing she sighed, gently dropping into her chair to stare out the window. She had thought maybe it was getting better. There had seemed to be little rays of sunshine and hope peeking through to her emotions. She could feel a lighter heaviness. Maybe one day she would be able to take a deep breath, hold it and slowly let it all out. Right now, it would still catch on her heartache and not allow her to take that full breath. As she started feeling that heaviness taking over again, she was startled by the sound of loud laughter. The high school aged kids were walking to school. The new high school had been built about a decade ago just blocks down the street. Some days they could hear the band practicing if the windows were open. There were three teenage boys walking in the middle of the street. One had picked up a small rock from the landscaping of the house next door. Ada's mouth dropped open when she saw the boy throw the rock with force and as her eyes followed the direction of the throw, she saw Oliver streak quickly around the side of another house. Two of the boys were laughing and slapping each other on the back. The third looked solemn. They turned to her house and looking right in the window at her, they pointed at her and started yelling at her house. She couldn't make out exactly what they were yelling, but she heard the words crazy and old.

It was at that moment that Stu rode up behind them on his scooter. Stu had been a friend of Charley's who lived several blocks away. Stu and Charley had worked together for decades and although they didn't do much outside of work, they were always glad to see each other. It had taken years for Ada to finally address him as Stu instead of his given name which was Stuart. Stu liked to drive around the neighborhood on his scooter at all hours of the day just to see what was going on. Even with her curtains closed, she could hear the sound of the small engine passing by most days. It brought her a temporary sense of ordinary and calmness to know that he was still out there checking on things and keeping the neighborhood in line. Today it brought a smile as she watched Stu like an animated cartoon yelling at the top of his gruff voice and chasing the boys down the street on his bright red scooter. Several minutes later, he passed by in the opposite direction, heading back to his home after his encounter with the boys. As he passed by Ada's house, he grinned and gave her a thumbs up.

CHAPTER 5

Feeling more energized than she had in recent memory, Ada decided to wash the inside of the window to match the cleanliness of the outside. She went into the kitchen and turned on the water to allow it the full minute it needed in order to get warm. She mixed her concoction of vinegar with just a dash of dish soap into the bucket of water. Reaching over to the radio, she turned the volume knob several degrees to the right. She was suddenly aware that her head was bobbing just a tiny bit to the tune on the radio. Pulling the old metal step ladder from its place next to the washing machine, she set up her small work station on the right side of the window. Working diligently and climbing up and down the three steps of the little ladder numerous times, she had washed and wiped dry the entire window. She was starting to feel a bit worn out. It had been a while since she had worked so hard but she was rewarded with a clear, streak free window. Stepping back to critique her work, she realized she had missed a spot in the top corner. Climbing to the top step, she reached up to catch the intersection she had missed the first time. It was just out of reach. Leaning in just a bit and stretching onto the tips of her toes, she finally reached it and was feeling satisfied when she felt her right foot slip off the step. The next thing she knew she was lying flat on the floor staring up at the ceiling. She held her breath for a second and slowly took inventory of her surroundings. Surprisingly, she realized she hadn't hit anything which was a relief. But as she tried to sit up, a shooting pain radiated from her shin. Looking down, she saw blood everywhere. Grabbing the extra rag she had brought in for wiping up water drips from her window cleaning, she pressed it to her leg. Feeling disappointed with herself for being careless, she made her way over to the chairs and used them to pull herself up. She felt light-headed and the pain in her leg was increasing. As much as she was dreading it, she made her way to the telephone. This was not going to be pleasant. She dialed the number.

After just one ring, the phone was answered. "Aunt A, what's wrong?"

"Now Joey, please don't make a fuss but could you come over here and tend to a tiny cut on my leg?" Ada asked with a calm that surprised her.

"What happened? Do you need an ambulance?" Joe asked with alarm. She didn't know it but he was already heading out of his office. Pushing the phone into his chest so she couldn't hear, he told his staff he would return as soon as he could. He ran to his car.

"Joey, of course I don't need an ambulance. I just need a little help. I'll see you when you get here."

"Ok. I'll be right there." Joe replied as he drove much too fast the short distance to her house.

When he arrived, he let himself into the back door. Ada was sitting at the table and raised her eyebrows at him. She said with some scolding, "Well, you couldn't have made it that fast by driving the speed limit."

One glance proved that this was not a tiny cut on her leg. "Aunt A, what happened?" He asked as he pulled the blood-soaked rag away from her leg. He revealed a deep gash several inches below her knee with a long and wide scrape for several more inches after it.

"I just lost my footing while I was cleaning the window." Ada said softly as she waited for his lecture.

He looked at her like she just told a bad joke. He shook his head and pursed his lips so he didn't say something he could not take back. He let out a deep breath and began, "How many times..."

Ada interrupted him, "I know. I know. I was feeling energetic and..." She shrugged.

"Was it that rickety old step ladder?" Joe asked quietly.

"Well, I have just one step ladder, Joseph, and it's not rickety." She huffed a little.

Trying to keep his thoughts under control, he finished cleaning up her wound. "I have several things to say. First, you are very lucky this wasn't worse. It's not good. But it could be worse. I will have to put several stitches in it. You should come to the office."

Ada started to voice her dissent. "I am not..."

Holding up a hand to stop her, he continued, "Second, I know you don't want to leave the house yet so I will do it here but you have to agree to let me send someone to come in and help you for a week or two. It's going to hurt and you will have to change the dressing every day. You had a tetanus shot several years ago, from this same ladder if I remember correctly so you are still covered for that."

Ada closed her mouth tight so she didn't make any comment as she glanced around the room and looked everywhere but in his direction. She tried not to grimace as he felt gingerly around her fresh wound.

Opening up his medical travel bag, Joe pulled out what he would need to disinfect the area along with the necessary supplies to stitch the gash. "I'm going to give you something to numb the area but it's still going to hurt. Are you ready?" After her nod of agreement, he started the process and it was over in no time. Hesitating to bring it up, he quietly started the discussion they had begun several times in the past years. "Aunt A, maybe it's time to think about going somewhere around people. What if you hadn't been able to make it to the phone?"

Instead of the usual quick response back, she thought through what to say. "Joey. I appreciate your concern. You know I do. But you check in with me every single night and I actually have been feeling better. I just got overly confident with the window washing. I could have been more careful. You know when you are doing something and for a split second, you think to yourself, 'this might be a bad idea' but you go ahead and do it anyway?"

Joe nodded with a slight smirk. "Everyone does that. I'm sure half my patients are there because of that very thing."

Appreciating his concession, she continued, "That's what happened today. I should have gotten off the stool and moved it over more. I was taking a short cut and I paid the price. I promise to be more careful. I don't want to go anywhere. I'm finally starting to see life around me again."

Having taken the seat next to her at the kitchen table after his stitching handiwork, he leaned over and patted her hand. Gesturing with his head toward the list on the table, he said, "I see you have your lists going again. Is this a special grocery list?" He was starting to feel more relaxed. He had been so nervous on his drive over here. Knowing the day would come eventually, he just couldn't stand the thought of anything happening to his aunt. She had been everything to him growing up. He didn't remember his mom. She had left when he was three. His dad couldn't, or more likely wouldn't, do what was necessary to care for him so he was sent to his Uncle Charley and Aunt Ada's home. It had been a wonderful place to grow up. He hadn't wanted for a thing and there was more than enough love to go around. He was grateful every day that they had taken him in. There was no telling where he would have ended up if they hadn't.

Ada responded to the grocery list, "Well, as a matter of fact, I had a notion to make you your favorite dish."

It had been over two years since she had made Charley and Joe's special request. Whenever there was a day of celebration and she asked them what they wanted for dinner, they always replied with the same answer, "Your lasagna."

Joe was overjoyed that she was feeling up to it again. It was unfortunate that after her fall, she wouldn't be able to prepare it for a while longer. "That sounds wonderful!" Joe said with enthusiasm. "But it will be a bit before you should be on your feet for longer than just a few minutes. How about when I come to check on you tomorrow, I bring some pasta from Valentini's".

With eyes lighting up, she answered, "That's a great idea. Thank you, Joey. We haven't had that for ages."

"I'm looking forward to it already. I'm going to get you some medicine for the pain. Expect it to swell a little and it will be sore. Don't be afraid to take something every four to six hours. Now don't argue with me, but I'm going to have someone from home health care come by mid-morning to check on you. They can help you get up and around and settled for the day." He gave Ada a look that she knew meant he wouldn't take no for an answer.

"Well, Joey, I'm not an invalid but if it makes you feel better, than that would be fine. Just for a day or two."

Surprised that she didn't protest, he didn't want to push his luck. "We'll see how it goes. Maybe a day or two, maybe longer. Where is Uncle Charley's old cane? You can use it to help you get around. You might be unsteady so don't take any chances."

"Joseph. Really. A cane? You aren't serious."

Joe just raised his eyebrows in a questioning look.

With a slight huff in her voice, she mumbled, "In the back of the coat closet."

Leaving for just a minute, he returned with the cane. He leaned it against the chair in the living room and helped move her from the kitchen in order to get her situated and as comfortable as possible before he had to leave. "Do you want the tv on? I'll get you a glass of water so you don't have to get up for a while."

Ada shooed him away. "Don't you have patients who are probably not very patiently waiting for you?"

"Right. Call me if you need anything at all." He leaned down to kiss her cheek and did his usual but not very subtle temperature check on her cheek and forehead with the back of his fingers. It was a sweet gesture of caring he had done since the day he graduated from medical school. It always made her heart swell just a little bit with pride and the feeling of being loved.

As Joe walked through the kitchen, she hollered out, "Lock the door behind you."

"Yes ma'am." He said with a grin. That had been their good bye for decades.

Several hours later, Ada was starting to feel uncomfortable. She did take some solace in being able to look out a nice clean window. Time was creeping by. The sun had returned after the morning storm and it appeared to be warming up again. Nice days were always a treat this time of year. You never knew if you would get a heat wave or a cold snap. It could start off the day one way and end the opposite. Ada usually kept the temperature in the house around 73 degrees, but this time of year she tried to keep the heat and air conditioning off. You could easily use both in the span of a day. Charley had never teased her when she said, "It needs to be off for a while to rest for the winter." She knew it was a silly thing to say but it made sense to her.

As her mind started wandering into the beginnings of sadness again, she was distracted by some movement outside. Feeling her mood lighten, she was pleased to see a familiar face. Ada just couldn't believe her eyes when she saw the young woman who had walked by the house for years. Not knowing exactly where she lived, Ada knew it had to be fairly close in order to walk by regularly. Ada remembered first seeing her in the evenings or on weekends walking with a young man. They would stop to visit if Charley and Ada were sitting on the front porch or working in the small yard. Their names were Ed and Colleen. Ed worked as a plumber and

Colleen worked in the office of the elementary school. They always had time to share a story or listen to a story. A few years later Ada noticed Colleen's size increasing by the month and then by the week. After several weeks of not seeing her, Ada was pleased to see her walking in the afternoons with a stroller. Little Levi was just about as adorable as any baby Ada had ever seen. Charley and Ada loved to peek into the stroller and comment on how big he was getting and hear stories about Levi's first time sleeping through the night or eating baby food. After cereal it was sweet potatoes which he loved then peas which he hated. They enjoyed hearing about his first tooth. His first word, "Ma". He would smile and drool and blow spit bubbles. And then Charley wasn't there anymore. And there were no more stories. Because, of course, the curtains were closed. The outside wasn't part of Ada's life any longer.

Now, as Ada leaned forward in her chair, she could not believe her eyes. Levi was walking right in front of Colleen. He was "helping" her push the stroller. They were right in front of the house when

Colleen put her hand on Levi's shoulder and told him to stop. She turned and looked in through that clean, clear window and smiled with big tears forming in her eyes. Colleen was as surprised to see the curtains open as Ada was to see them standing on the sidewalk. Her hand come up as three fingers covered her mouth and several tears rolled down her cheeks. She said something to Levi as she pointed to the window. Ada smiled and waved. Levi's small hand waved a big arc back and forth in the air. Colleen took a few steps to the front of the stroller and reached in for the tiny bundle wrapped in a blanket. She held the baby so Ada could see the tiny little face. Ada nodded her head and clapped her hands with a big smile. Colleen put the baby back into the stroller, Levi and Colleen waved again and continued on their way. Everyone involved had a lighter, happier heart after the non-conventional reunion.

Ada had a strong desire to go outside to hear a story. She longed to call out Colleen's name and ask her to stop so Ada could see the baby and Levi up close. Not even considering her new injury as a deterrent, she felt the battle inside. The strong desire to go outside was overpowered by an even stronger need to stay in her confining cocoon of safety. Hearing stories and seeing growing children without Charley by her side seemed too hard to imagine. But to be honest, Ada felt encouraged that for the first time she actually had a desire to go outside. Maybe she was getting better. How do you move on from perfect? Do you start at the bottom? Her leg starting to pulse. Ada stared at her leg and thought that she was glad to feel something other than her wounded heart pounding a pulse through her whole body. The pounding that made her want to curl up in darkness to absorb the pain of the memories and her sorrow.

CHAPTER 6

It had been a surprisingly restful night. Maybe it was the pain medicine for her leg, but Ada felt good when she woke the next day. It was a bit of a shock, however, when she decided to swing her legs out of the covers to get out of bed. Her whole body was stiff. As she thought about it, she was actually thankful that she could move at all. That was a pretty hard fall off the stool. She made her way into the kitchen, turned on the radio and glanced out the window over the sink. No wonder she felt a chill. There had been a dusting of snow. She slowly hobbled her way into the living room and opened the curtains to a thin blanket of white covering the sidewalk, streets and rooftops. The grass still stood defiantly sticking it's blades up wherever it could. Patches of white mixed in. Ada stood staring at it for several minutes. The leaves were still holding on as they continued to change more beautiful as they waited to finish dying so they could release their grip on the branches that had held them since last spring. The first snow was always calming and exciting at the same time. It was peaceful and seemed to make everything quiet as it absorbed the sounds in the air.

Ada cracked a small smile as she noticed tiny cat footprints going from the sidewalk, up her steps, and disappearing once on the porch which had not received the gift of snow because of the slightly sloping cover of a roof. Oliver must have been out hunting for breakfast.

Her eyes strayed to the house across the street. She stared at the broken window upstairs. It had been quiet over there for several days. She hadn't seen the little boy inside or out. The dirty, old truck with the angry man hadn't been parked in front of the house either. Telling herself to mind her own business, that it was all none of her concern, she still couldn't help the occasional drifting of her thoughts to the sweet boy. She worried about him being alone, hungry, sick, scared, hurt, cold. She was about to start pacing when her discomfort reminded her to get about her day. Wandering into the kitchen to make her toast and egg, she discovered that no matter how hard she tried to stop herself or distract herself, her mind kept going back across the street. Should she call someone? Who would she call? If Charley were here, he would know what to do. Certainly she was making too much of it. He was probably just one of those many children who spent every other week with a different parent or something.

Ada placed her dishes in the sink instead of washing them like usual. As she went into the bedroom to make the bed, she realized it was quite difficult to move around. She felt something on her leg and looking down, saw a small amount of blood trickling down toward her ankle. Feeling frustrated but also concerned that if something happened to her wound, she would likely have to go somewhere to be cared for at Joey's insistence. She left everything to sit in her chair and elevate her leg for a bit.

The peaceful quiet and beauty of the light snow was quickly diminishing. A few cars had driven down the road and left tire tracks through the melting blanket. A chickadee flew past and landed on a branch of the tree. It then made the short journey from the branch to the porch then finally to the window ledge and peered into the window at her. Ada's gaze went from the beautiful bird who was twitching its head back and forth probably trying to figure out its own reflection in the window, to the small stack of books on the top of the small bookcase against the wall. Right on the top of the pile was the book about birds from the area. How many days had she and Charley paged through it looking to see if they had just spotted a new bird? They kept a pencil next to it just in case they lucked out and got to check off a new box from the index in the back. In the rare cases when they did see something new, they would figure out the date and pencil it in too. Once Charley retired, they usually had to go to the calendar on the wall to find out the date. The days all blended together only needing to be remembered if there was an appointment of some kind written in the square on the calendar. These days, Ada didn't have any idea what day it was. Or really even what month. But she didn't care. She didn't have a reason to know. Joey had replaced the calendar on the wall the past couple years. Every month on the first, he would fold over the outdated month to reveal the new one. He always made several comments about the picture on the current month. He was always trying to get her at least a little interested in things again. Last year's calendar was flowers, this year was barns. They were nice. They were fine.

Bruce drove by and since he was now expecting her curtains to be open, he slowed way down, almost coming to a stop. He rolled down the window, turned toward her and wrapped his arms around himself to give an exaggerated shiver as if to let her know how cold it was out there. Then he chuckled. She remembered his chuckle and could almost hear it in her mind. He rolled up the window and beeped twice as he continued down the road.

Shortly after, the school children were running past. They tried their best to slide with their shoes on the snow but it wasn't slippery. They tried to scoop tiny bits of almost melted snow into their hands for a snowball but it dissolved before they could achieve their goal. Their faces were bright and eyes were shining from the cold dampness in the air. Apparently it brought with it energy because instead of going into Jeannie's house, they stayed outside and chased each other in a game of tag until the bus arrived.

As the high school boys walked by today, they were quieter. They were walking at a quick pace with their heads down and their hands buried in their pockets. Ada wondered why they didn't carry backpacks. How did they do homework without books? She watched them as they made their way down the now snow-free road. The one boy who had seemed uncomfortable with the other two yelling words at her the other day, turned his head ever so slightly to glance in at her. As he did, he stood a little taller, lifted his head up, and seemed to be more alert.

Ada sucked in a deep breath then released it with a huge sigh. It was going to be a long day. She realized that when she was in the kitchen, she hadn't turned the radio on. Maybe that was good. Just as often as a song can make you happy and fill you with good memories, there can be a song that brings with it memories that whether they are good or bad will still tug down the optimism of the day. Memories are great until you realize that they are only that. Memories made in the past with no new ones to look forward to in the future. Right now, at this time of day, Charley would be sitting in his chair working on the crossword. He would either be asking her questions, humming the tune on the radio or a tune that was playing in his head. Ada looked over toward his chair. She wished for a moment that she hadn't taken the pain medicine with breakfast. It would be better to feel her leg throbbing. With another loud sigh, she looked out at the house across the street again. At least it would give her something to think about other than how many hours it would be before she could go to bed for the night.

Ada was feeling restless and not sure how to proceed with her day. It took her by surprise when a car slowly rolled up in front of her house and came to a stop. A woman got out of the car and opened the back door to retrieve a bag from the back seat. She started walking up the front sidewalk. Ada had completely forgotten that Joey was going to send someone from home health care over this morning. She half thought he had been joking about that. Ada had to grab Charley's cane to help pull herself up from the chair. She had just stood up when there was a knock on the front door. Moving slowly to the woman's knock, Ada called out, "Coming."

Opening the door, she was greeted by a friendly, smiling face whose warm eyes sparkled with happiness. The woman opened the screen door and stepped inside. Ada could see her quickly assess Ada's health with her eyes. She set her bag from the back seat on the floor inside the door as she quickly kicked off her shoes. Grabbing Ada by the elbow, she started steering her back toward her chair. She spoke with a soft, caring voice, "Hello, Ada. My name is Rebecca. I'm with home health care and I assume you have been expecting me." Ada nodded slightly. Rebecca continued speaking as she helped Ada lower herself back into the chair. "I understand you took a fall off a stool yesterday that required stitches. Do you mind if I take a look at it?" Ada gave her consent and Rebecca knelt down in front of her and gently started folding up Ada's pants leg. "I see you have had a bit of bleeding this morning. Let's see what's going on under here." She was so tender that Ada could hardly feel the bandage being peeled back. Rebecca felt around the wound and the ever-increasing bruise. She was surprised that this frail looking woman didn't even flinch as she did her examination. Rebecca got up and retrieved her bag from where she had deposited it upon arrival. Coming back over, she once again knelt down to clean up the wound and bandage it back up. "I think maybe you were just on your feet for too long at one time. That's what caused the slight bleeding. Did you try to do your normal morning activities today?" Rebecca asked even though she already knew the answer.

"Well, yes. I suppose I did. I tried. I wasn't able to get much done." Ada replied. She was feeling anxious about having someone in the house. No one had been in here except Joey. She didn't know if she was ready. However, she supposed there wasn't much of a choice. And this person did seem very nice.

"That's why I'm here. I came to help you do some of the things you shouldn't be doing until your leg is healed." Rebecca stood back up and noticed that Ada's eyes were looking over at the chair an arm's length from where she was sitting. She knew it must be her husband's chair. It had been in her file that her husband had passed on just about two years ago. Not wanting to upset Ada by invading what she expected was still her husband's space, Rebecca asked if she would like to continue their conversation at the kitchen table.

With relief, Ada quickly agreed. It didn't go without acknowledgment that most people wouldn't have been that considerate. Ada was feeling more comfortable with this new acquaintance with each passing minute. After being helped to the kitchen chair, Rebecca was filled in on Ada's daily routine and what she felt was acceptable to allow Rebecca to do for her.

Rebecca asked tentatively, "Do you mind if I ask you a few questions about what your daily life was like when your husband was still here?"

61

Ada started wringing her hands together in her lap without even noticing the nervous habit. She had never been one to be disagreeable or uncooperative so she answered, "Okay."

"I do know that his name was Charley and he has been gone for two years. Yes?" Rebecca started as she leaned back as if to give Ada more space.

"Yes." Ada looked at her hands in her lap and quickly quit clasping them. Instead, she crossed her arms in front of her in a defensive manner.

"What did you do when Charley was here? Did you always do things together or did you have some hobbies that you did separately?"

Swallowing twice before being able to answer, she felt like a hundred things flashed through her mind in an instant. "We did most things together."

"Can you think of anything you did by yourself? Any hobbies? Crafts?"

"Well, I did crochet baby hats."

Smiling approvingly, Rebecca replied, "That's so nice. Do you still make them?"

Creasing her brow, Ada answered, "No. I guess I don't."

"Would you like to start again? Do you have what you need?"

"I haven't really thought about it. I suppose I could do that. They probably could still use them. If I have any yarn, it would be in the extra bedroom closet on the floor, on the right, inside the door, in a canvas bag."

Rebecca smiled at her precise memory. "Do you want me to go check to see if you have any?"

Thinking about it for just a moment, Ada nodded her head and smiled ever so slightly. "Sure. Thank you."

In just short of a minute due to the excellent description of where to look, Rebecca came back with the canvas bag. Unfortunately, it was almost empty. There was just one lone half skein.

Feeling surprisingly disappointed, Ada reached for her pen and note pad that were still on the table from yesterday. "I will add it to my list."

"Excellent!" Rebecca was feeling light-hearted. "How about reading? Do you enjoy reading?"

Ada got a thoughtful expression on her face. She didn't answer.

"Is that something you and Charley did together?" Rebecca asked quietly.

"Yes. Charley loved mysteries. We would go to the library and pick out one or two at a time. Then we would take turns reading out loud one chapter at a time. We would discuss between chapters what we thought would happen or who we thought was the suspect. He was always much better at it than me. He guessed right almost every time." It felt good to talk about Charley to someone other than just Joey.

Rebecca could see a glimmer in Ada's eyes when she talked about Charley. She imagined that it used to be a spark dulled by loss. Maybe she could help her get it back. "Would you want to get a book to read?"

Ada looked slightly panicked. "Oh no. I don't want to go to the library. I don't want to go anywhere yet."

Rebecca leaned across the table and put her hand on Ada's arm. "No. We don't have to go anywhere. Let me show you something." She pulled her laptop out of her bag and opened it. After clicking on the keyboard several times, she turned the computer around and watched Ada's eyebrows raise in disbelief.

Leaning forward to look closer at the computer screen, Ada could make out the book covers of numerous books, some of which she recognized. "What is this?" she asked.

Rebecca explained the library website. "Do you want to get one or two?"

"Really? I just check it out? How do I get it?"

"They will deliver it to you. Or I could go pick it up for you. Here, press this button and you can scroll down to see what else they have. How about if you look for a while and I will wash up those couple dishes and go make your bed?"

"Oh no, dear. You don't have to do that. I will get to it."

Getting up from the table, Rebecca reached over and rubbed Ada's shoulder a few times. "Ada. I'm here to help you. I would like to do those things. Is that ok with you?"

Feeling conflicted between embarrassment at needing help and appreciation for the offer, Ada nodded her head and said with gratitude, "Thank you, Rebecca."

Several hours after her arrival, Rebecca left Ada with a positive attitude, two library books to be delivered, a clean kitchen, a made-up bed and the anticipation of seeing her again tomorrow. It was nice to have something to look forward to.

CHAPTER 7

Joe arrived shortly after six o'clock. He came in the back door loaded down with enough food from Valentini's for the whole neighborhood. Ada had set the table and even made up some of her famous sweet tea. She wouldn't tell Joe that she had used decaffeinated tea. He wouldn't know the difference and she didn't want to be the reason he couldn't sleep well tonight.

He could tell instantly that she was feeling better. "Did you have a good day?" he asked as he set the bags on the counter and leaned down to kiss her cheek, checking her temperature with the slightest brush of his fingers.

She smiled at him as she took her place at the table. She started unloading the bags. "I did. Did you get enough food? Wash your hands."

Laughing, he obediently walked over to the sink and started soaping up. "I might have gotten a little carried away. I didn't eat much for lunch. So, when I ordered our supper, everything sounded so good I couldn't help myself. Plus, this way we can both have left overs tomorrow."

"That sounds like a well thought out plan," she agreed.

As they were heaping their plates with the delicious smelling food, there was a knock on the front door. Joe looked at Ada with a question on his face. "Who could that be?" He walked to the front door and swung it open expecting to have to turn away someone selling something. Instead, there was a beautiful lady who took several steps back after seeing his looming presence filling the doorway. She looked quickly around her to make sure she was at the right house. "Can I help you?" Joe asked in a pleasant voice.

"I'm sorry to bother you. Is Ada home?" the woman asked timidly.

From the other room, Ada hollered, "Rebecca, is that you?" Ada hobbled around the doorway of the kitchen. "Come in, please. Joey, this is Rebecca, my home health care nurse." Ada continued across the small room to Joe. "Rebecca, this is my nephew, Joey."

They shook hands. "Nice to meet you," they both said at the same time.

"Rebecca, we were just sitting down to supper. Will you join us? Joey brought enough for a village." Ada asked with enthusiasm.

Turning pink in her cheeks, Rebecca held up a small bag. "No, thank you. I just wanted to drop this off for you. I had to stop by the store so I picked up some yarn for you while I was there. I'm sorry to interrupt your meal."

Ada put her arm around Rebecca's. "Help me back to the table, will you?" Ada asked sweetly.

Turning to Joe, she addressed him politely, "Joey, set another place at the table."

Rebecca helped Ada back to her seat at the table. "No. I'm sorry. I came at a bad time."

Ada asked with genuine concern, "Do you have a family you have to get home to? You shouldn't have made a special trip. Although I am glad to see you and am very thankful for the yarn."

Feeling awkward, Rebecca hesitated before stating, "No. No one at home. I don't want to intrude on your time."

Ada laughed light-heartedly. "Don't be silly. We are happy for the company. Aren't we Joey? Please, sit." She said motioning to the chair next to her where Joe had set the extra place setting.

Not able to politely answer any other way, Joe said, "Of course. Please, join us." His aunt seemed more enthused than he had seen her since the police had come to deliver the bad news.

Ada pointed to the pitcher of tea. "Would you like some tea? I made it special for our fancy restaurant dinner."

Joey encouraged her by grabbing the pitcher and holding it up for approval. "Aunt A is famous for her tea."

Rebecca held up her hand in a negative gesture. "No, thank you, if I have caffeine this time of day, I won't sleep a wink."

Ada's face lit up and she declared, "I know dear, but just between you and me," she sheepishly glanced at Joe out of the corner of her eyes, "I made it with decaf tea so it's ok."

"Really? Well then, fill it up! That sounds wonderful." She didn't look directly at Joe as he poured her glass full of the special-made brew. "Thank you so much." Rebecca stated to both.

It was quiet for several minutes as Rebecca filled her plate and they all filled their mouths. Ada was the first to break the silence. "Well, obviously this is delicious since we are so busy enjoying it that we haven't taken a breath to speak." Turning to Rebecca she asked, "Rebecca, I talked a lot about myself today, but I didn't really get a chance to ask about you. Tell us about you. What's your story?"

Not feeling comfortable being the center of attention, Rebecca was brief but all-encompassing in her reply. "Umm, well, you know where I work. I have worked with the company for nine years. I recently re-located here from Tulsa. I have two children. My daughter, Sarah, is 22 and just started her last year of college in Kansas. My son, William, I call him Billy, is 19 and is in his second year of college in Arkansas.

71

They are both planning to be high school teachers. I love dog and cats but I don't have any pets. And, let's see," she looked up to the ceiling as if thinking "my favorite color is navy blue and I love Italian food." She raised a breadstick in the air as if toasting a drink and took a bite, chewing slowly hoping to avoid talking any more.

Ada couldn't help herself. She blurted out, "Are you married?" She looked over at Joe who looked down into his plate with just a hint of a smirk on the corners of his mouth. He looked back up and made eye contact with Rebecca. He was surprised at how curious he was to hear her answer. She noticed how the corners of his eyes wrinkled up when he smiled.

Swallowing her mouthful of breadstick, she reached over and grabbed her tea glass to wash it down. She lightly cleared her throat before stating, "No. Divorced. About 15 years."

Ada made a hmm sound which neither Joe nor Rebecca could decipher. Then she continued on talking about seeing Colleen, Levi and the baby walking by this morning. Joe told them about rumors of a new restaurant opening in town. Rebecca relayed a story about the close call when a young girl ran out in front of a car in the parking lot of the store where she had been buying Ada's yarn. They discussed the weather forecast for tomorrow which was expected to be much warmer than today and finished up with the news coverage of a flu bug that was spreading through the state.

The early evening had gone by much faster than they realized. Rebecca saw the time on the clock radio and pushed back her chair to get up. She reached over to start picking up the empty plates. As she quickly piled the dishes into a stack, she asked, "Ada, would you like me to look at your leg and help you get settled for the night?"

"Oh, thank you dear, but Joey can do that. Do you want to take some leftovers home? The Tupperware containers are right there in the cupboard by the fridge."

Smiling her appreciation at the offer, Rebecca shook her head. "I have a long day tomorrow so I probably won't be home to eat it. I would be happy to pack it up for you though." She set the dishes on the countertop by the sink and pulled out several containers. Joe had gotten up and turned on the water, getting the dish soap out from under the sink. As he waited for the water to get hot, he put the pitcher of what remained of the tea in the refrigerator. "Joey, thank you for providing such a nice, unexpected dinner for me tonight."

Joe felt his smile reach his eyes. No one called him Joey except his aunt. He realized that he didn't mind. He actually kind of enjoyed it. "It was my pleasure. Thank you for taking such great care of Aunt A. Sometimes she can be a bit of a handful." He teased Ada with a wink.

"Joseph. Honestly. You're the handful." Ada replied with mock annoyance.

In a matter of a few short minutes, Joe and Rebecca had the kitchen cleaned up and Rebecca was heading to the front door.

Reaching over to shake Joe's hand, Rebecca shook it warmly and said, "Thank you both for such a lovely dinner and conversation. I don't know when

I've had such a pleasant evening." She reached over and gave Ada a brief hug that seemed completely natural. It felt as if she had known them for years.

Ada nodded her agreement. "I'm so glad you could join us. I'll see you in the morning."

"Drive safe." Joe said as she walked out the front door. They both watched her get into her car and drive away.

Joe caught Ada staring at him. "What?" He asked as he closed the door, locking it and turning to take Ada's arm to help her to her chair.

"Nothing. That was a nice time. You two seemed to get along well. She's a pretty gal, isn't she." Ada said it more as a statement than a question. "And so sweet."

"Really? I hadn't noticed." Joe said with a touch of banter. Changing the subject to avoid any more questions, he asked, "How about I check your leg and help you get settled in for the night?" After making sure Ada had everything she would need and that she was comfortable, he made his way to the back door.

"Lock the door behind you."

"Yes ma'am."

Ada didn't know it, but Joe did have trouble falling asleep that night. And it obviously didn't have anything to do with the tea.

CHAPTER 8

Waking to the sound of birds outside the window always used to make Ada happy. She hadn't heard them for several years. She realized this morning that maybe she just hadn't been listening. Not wanting a repeat of yesterday's wound bleeding, she decided to take it easy. Making just a piece of toast and skipping the egg, she decided to pass on the pain medicine since she was feeling much better. Turning the radio on, she quickly started humming along with the familiar tune filling the room. She got dressed with more energy than usual. She was actually looking forward to what the day had in store. Opening the curtains, she was greeted with bright, early morning sunshine. There was something about the sun this time of day. It didn't bring with it heat as much as just a feeling of internal warmth. It felt hopeful and promising.

Noticing the bag of yarn on the countertop, she grabbed it along with her crocket hook and took her seat in the living room to await her new routine of outdoor visitors as they passed by on their daily travels. Ada pulled out the skeins of yarn and admired their lovely, pastel colors. There was a minty sea green and a color that she couldn't decide if she would call it dandelion or daffodil. Delighted to have to make a choice for something so enjoyable, she chose to start with the green. It took a while for her hands to loosen up and remember the relaxing movements of taking a bulk of yarn and transforming it into a tiny, warm hat for an infant.

Ada was enjoying the time spent working on a project while bouncing her toes once in a while to the music playing in the background. She waved to Bruce and watched the kids on their journeys to school imagining they would be excited that it was a Friday so the weekend was nearly here. Making slow but efficient progress on her new past time, she was concentrating on crocheting when she heard a car door slam. Raising her glance to see the source of the slam, she was surprised to see someone walking up to her front door. As she made eye contact with the individual, they smiled and raised the two books they were carrying in their hand up into the air. Ada set her crocheting on Charley's chair and made it as quickly as possible to the door. The book deliverer was patiently waiting for the door to open and handed them to Ada with a short conversation about enjoying them before continuing on to the next delivery. Ada couldn't believe that she had looked on a computer yesterday and the books were here already. Was it due to being from such a small town that everyone knew she hadn't checked a book out of the library for so long? Whatever the reason, Ada was happy to have them in her hand and by looking at the pictures on the covers, she decided which one to start first. In her opinion, it was untrue that you didn't judge a book by its cover. The one she chose just looked more interesting.

Usually, the days seemed to stretch out in front of her without any meaning. Today, however, she was excited to once again be faced with multiple options of activities. Deciding to set aside crocheting for a bit, she opened to the first chapter of the more interesting looking book. She had hardly finished a page when her mind started wandering and she couldn't help but glance out the window. With each page she read, she spent more and more time wondering about the boy across the street. Where did he go? People didn't just disappear. Well, except in these mystery books. There had been no activity at that house in several days. Ada felt disappointed at the thought that maybe they had moved along. She would have made sure to wave a nice good-bye to the boy.

Not being able to get into the novel, she set it aside and made her way into the kitchen. She turned off the radio. It had gone from being a nice distraction to now just being noise. Putting on some water to boil for tea, she was welcoming the idea of Rebecca coming. Yesterday, the thought of a stranger coming into her home made her nervous. Today she was looking forward to it. Funny how just one day could make someone seem like a friend instead of a stranger. It was almost time for her arrival so Ada took two cups out the cupboard and paced the floor a few times waiting for the water. She was trying to determine if her leg was feeling 50 percent better or

60. Just as she finished pouring the water over the teabags, she heard a light rap on the front door. With quicker steps than usual, she made it to the door in short order. Rebecca's cheerful greeting was just what Ada needed.

Ada stepped aside to let Rebecca enter and remove her shoes. She said, "I just made some tea. Would you like a cup knowing that I already made you one?"

With a light chuckle, Rebecca replied, "Well, I suppose I could be talked into it." Walking past the chairs, she noticed the start of the tiny green hat. "It looks like you have already begun your project. Do you mind if I look at it?"

"Sure. You picked such nice colors. I decided on the green to start with. I think it will look quite nice."

Picking up the few rows of the start of the little head warmer, she wrapped it so the ends touched. "It's hard to remember my kids being this small." Rebecca stated with a tinge of nostalgia. Setting it back down she noticed the books on the small table between the chairs. "You received your books already?" she asked with surprise.

"I know. They must be very efficient. I started one of them but can't quite seem to get that interested."

Rebecca nodded her head. "I understand that. Sometimes I just can't concentrate enough to follow what's going on. No matter how good it is. It looks like you have been busy since I saw you last." They both took a seat at the table to sip on the tea that Ada had just steeped.

Ada agreed. "It seems like I have a lot more options since yesterday. Thank you again for the yarn and for helping me find something to read. It will help to pass the time."

Rebecca smiled. "I'm glad to help. How is your leg feeling today?"

"Oh, really much better. I haven't looked at it but I can tell it's healing."

"When we finish our tea, I'll take a peek. Is there anything else you would like to do today?"

Ada wasn't one to ask for help but she did indeed have something on her mind. With some hesitation, she reached up and ran her fingers through her thinning hair. Slightly embarrassed, she said, "As you can see, I haven't been to the hair dresser for quite some time. I usually just trim my hair myself. I do know it doesn't look very kept. Do you suppose you could help me trim it just a touch? Now, mind you, I won't be a bit offended if that is asking too much."

Rebecca's eyes sparkled with the reflection of the kitchen light over the table. "Ada, it would be my pleasure. I used to cut my kid's hair because they wouldn't sit still for anyone else and I also cut my dad's hair all the time. I'm a little out of practice but I used to be pretty good at it."

"That would be wonderful. There is an old sheet we can set on the floor to catch the hair clippings and I will go get the scissors I use. They probably aren't the best, but they get the job done."

Happy to see Ada's enthusiasm, Rebecca slowed her down a bit. "How about if you finish your tea first and I check on how your leg is doing?"

"Yes. That would be best I suppose." Ada let Rebecca remove the dressing to check her wound.

"It's looking much better. I can tell that you have been doing well resting it." Giving it a gentle cleaning and then covering it again, they made small talk until it was taken care of. "Do you want me to wash your hair in the sink before we start cutting?"

"That would really feel nice. I'll grab a towel and the shampoo when I get the scissors." Ada headed to the bathroom to retrieve the items. Rebecca looked around the tiny, tidy kitchen. Next to the door going out to the back yard, was a small, tall table that was conveniently positioned to be the spot to drop a few items when entering. She imagined the car keys and possibly Ada's purse used to have a permanent place there, although they weren't there now. There was a picture frame that sat at an angle toward the back. Taking a closer look, Rebecca noticed that it was a photo of Ada and she imagined it must be Ada's husband, Charley, standing next to her with his arm around her shoulder. On the other side of Ada was a much younger version of Joey. Ada's arm clutching his at the crook of his elbow as if he was about to escort her somewhere. They were all smiling genuine, happy smiles that reached all the way to their eyes. Rebecca leaned in a little to get a closer look to see if he had the start of the wrinkles around his smiling eyes at an earlier age. She heard Ada enter the kitchen and quickly stepped away from the table turning her attention back to the task at hand.

Ada didn't say anything but was amused by the look of guilty embarrassment that crossed Rebecca's face at being caught looking at the photo. Who wouldn't look? Joey was quite a handsome man and his character and heart made him even more attractive. Ada never could figure out why no one had snatched him up. She did believe that it was better that he was alone rather than being with the wrong person. That would be much worse. He seemed to enjoy his life and his work. She sure would love to see him find a nice gal to settle down with though.

Putting the towel around her shoulders, Ada leaned over the sink and let the warm water run over her head. Rebecca was accustomed to this procedure so it took just minutes before Ada was sitting in the chair with the sheet underneath and the clipping about to commence. Rebecca ran her fingers through the wet hair, pulling it out and away from Ada's head. "How much are you wanting trimmed off?"

Ada made a few gestures with her mouth moving it from side to side and pursing her lips together as if deep in thought. "I don't know. What do you think?"

"Well, do you want it to look like you got your hair cut or hardly enough so you can't really tell? I can just kind of straighten up the edges. What are you in the mood for?" Rebecca asked.

"You know what? I'm feeling adventurous. Let's really make a change. Clip away. If I change my mind, it will always grow back." Ada gave one solid nod of her head and felt comfortable with her decision.

Laughing and feeling good about the confidence that Ada had in her abilities, Rebecca hoped she wouldn't disappoint her as she gathered the first bit of hair and snipped off a rather long section. Joking with her, Rebecca stated, "Well, if you hate it, you have the yarn to make yourself a hat to cover it up until it grows out."

They made small talk while the process continued. They discussed the weather, their favorite comfort foods for cold winter nights and what Rebecca thought of living in the small town. Before they knew it, the final touch up was complete. Rebecca took a few steps back to admire her work. "Not bad if I do say so myself," she claimed.

"I can't wait to see it." Ada said as she pushed herself up from the kitchen chair. She headed to the bathroom to check it out in the mirror as Rebecca started cleaning up the stray hair pieces that had flown around and landed in random places. Ada hollered from the other room, "I love it!" She walked back into the kitchen and rewarded Rebecca with a glowing smile. "I feel like I've been to the salon. You could be a professional. Thank you so much."

With eyes on the floor, Rebecca quietly stated, "You're welcome. I've missed doing it so thank you for trusting me enough to pick up the scissors again."

"Do you live too far away from your parents to cut your dad's hair anymore?" Ada asked with sympathy.

"No. My parents were killed in a car accident six years ago. I haven't had any practice since then. I should have told you that you were my guinea pig to see if I still had any ability. I haven't felt comfortable enough to try until today." She smiled sadly.

"Oh, honey, I'm so sorry. I'm glad I got to be your trial run. You passed with flying colors." Ada leaned over to give her a quick, tight hug.

Trying to change the subject to lighten the mood, Rebecca asked, "What sounds good for lunch? I can whip up something if you're hungry."

"Would you eat some leftovers from last night with me?" Ada asked.

"That sounds good. It was so nice of you to include me in your dinner especially on such short notice." Rebecca said with a hint of embarrassment at the interruption.

"Well, Joey and I both enjoyed your company." Looking her squarely in the eyes, Ada said, "Maybe we can do it again sometime. The three of us."

Ada enjoyed the slightly long pause and Rebecca breaking eye contact to look away with just a hint of color in her face. Rebecca overly cheerfully stated, "Well, maybe we can." Then she quickly turned to get the leftovers out of the refrigerator while noticing her heart beating a touch faster.

The time had flown by and Rebecca was getting ready to leave for the day. She had helped Ada with several things around the house in order to make it easier over the weekend since she wouldn't be back until Monday. As she was heading to the door to put her shoes on, she was startled by a flash by the front window. Walking over to take a look, she couldn't help but laugh out loud to see a white cat chasing a squirrel around the base of a tree then continue in circles while looking up to see if it would be worth it to get stuck up in those branches. The squirrel was crouched high on his perch almost seeming to laugh at the cat. Sitting down and staring up into the leaves as if he was ready to sit all day in a waiting game for the squirrel to come down, he jumped in surprise as the squirrel took off and jumped from the end of a tree limb onto the roof. Looking disgusted and sticking his nose in the air as if he had been getting bored with it anyway, he strolled onto the porch and hopped up onto the rocking chair. His tiny, shiny nose glistened just an inch from the window as he stared inside to see what was going on.

Ada called out a warning. "Don't you dare put your slimy nose on my clean window!"

Everybody knows you never dare a cat. Sure enough, he leaned forward that final inch and placed his wet little button right into the glass. He pulled back and stared in at her.

"Well, you little bugger! See if I feed you again." Ada said as she turned to Rebecca. "Can you believe the nerve?"

Rebecca could hold her bubbling laughter no longer. It spilled out before she had any control. After a full minute of laughing which Ada joined in after the first five seconds, Rebecca stated between breaths of chuckles, "That was the funniest thing I have seen in ages. He did it on purpose. I know he did."

"That's what I get for being nice to him. I gave him some food the other day but I think he wants to come in and check the place out. He may be hunting for a warm place to stay over the winter."

"If you want to encourage him, I can pick up some cat food. He might be nice company." Rebecca said thinking it might be nice for Ada to have a reason to talk when no one was around.

"Well, he's not coming inside. But it might be nice to give him some good food once in a while. I don't know how his hunting skills are outside. From what I've seen, I don't think he gets many birds or squirrels. Maybe I can make a little shelter somewhere to provide him with protection from the weather this winter. I'll ask Joey to help me." She chuckled.

As Rebecca left the house, the cat tried to sneak inside. Ada reprimanded him, "Oliver. It's not going to happen." Oliver looked at her with eager, imploring little eyes. Gosh, he was cute. Hesitating for only a second, Ada closed the door before she allowed herself to change her mind.

Ada took a seat in the comfort of her living room chair. It had been a delightful day so far. Soon she could watch the kids get off the bus and scramble home to begin their plans. She debated between reading and crocheting. She felt a bit light-hearted with the sun streaming through the window and several choices of activities. Picking up her crocheting, she began the task of starting a new row leading closer to a complete hat to warm a baby's head. She had hardly gotten started when she noticed someone coming up her sidewalk. Glancing out the window, she was surprised to see Cynthia. She carried a book and a large travel size mug of water. She walked past the door and toward the rocking chair. Looking into the window, she said loudly through the panes of glass, "Care if I join you?"

Ada smiled and nodded.

Cynthia took a seat and set her water on the dusty little table. She slowly rocked back and forth as she opened up to where her bookmark held her place. It was her way of spending time with Ada without pushing her past her comfort level of allowing people into her space yet.

Ada felt her eyes moisten with the knowledge that very few people were as considerate and caring as her dear friend. She felt that she didn't deserve the patience and understanding that Cynthia had showered on her every day for over two years. How could she ever express her thankfulness? Cynthia had never given up on her. This had indeed been the best day she had experienced since her loss.

Ada went to bed that night feeling more optimistic about the next day than she had dared to imagine would ever be possible again. She just knew she fell asleep with a smile on her face.

CHAPTER 9

Halfway through the night, Ada woke from a dream. It took a minute to realize she was awake. She loved dreaming about Charley. It made it seem like she had just gotten to see him. Usually, they were pleasant dreams of places they had been or of times just spent being together. Tonight, in her dream, she was scared.

She had been walking on a construction beam high up in the air. She couldn't tell where it was attached to anything and she felt like she was going to fall. It was what she imagined it would be like for a circus performer to walk a tight rope. She felt herself getting tense. If she breathed too hard, she knew she would fall. She put her arms out to her sides to try to balance herself. She remembered seeing on tv shows or reading in books that you must not look down. She tried to focus only on the beam ahead of her. If she started walking, where would she end up? The beam just went on and on with no end in sight. Feeling herself swaying to one side, she quickly tried to balance back to center.

Breathing hard through her mouth, she took a few deep gulps of air and then swallowed several times. Blinking to clear her vision, she stared at the beam and put her right foot forward and felt around with her toes. She started leaning too far over again but was afraid to pull her foot back.

Suddenly Charley was next to her. He reached for her hand to steady her. He looked her in the eyes. Smiling his warm, gentle smile, he said, "Don't worry, Ada Grace. I gotcha."

Ada felt a tender tug on her heart. "Don't let go, Charley. I don't know how to balance without you."

Charley shook his head slowly. "You are doing great. You are the toughest gal I know."

"Charley, please don't leave me. I'll fall. I can't..."

There was a loud crash and everything was gone. It was always bittersweet to wake from a dream involving Charley. After a full minute to feel awake from such a deep sleep, Ada realized that the noise she heard in her dream was actually some commotion outside. After the crashing noise that initially woke her up, she could have sworn she heard loud music. Feeling frustrated at the length of time it now took to get out of bed, she eventually made it to the window. She pulled back one of the curtains about a foot from its tight enclosure in the middle of the window and peeked through the opening. Ada was surprised to see that it was snowing quite heavily. She then noticed the blue pick-up truck parked once again across the street. Upon closer inspection, she realized that it had been parked at a strange angle and the front tire was up on the curb. The light was on in what she assumed was the living room. Quickly she gazed at the upstairs, cracked window. Of course, it was silly to think the boy would have arrived home tonight. It was the middle of the night. He would be sound asleep somewhere. Letting the curtain fall back into place, she made her way back to bed. Tossing and turning the rest of the night, the feeling of optimism she had when she went to bed was now long gone.

Ada woke from her restless sleep to the sound of a snow plow. It seemed mighty early in the season to have snow plows out already. The air in the house had that slight chill and deafening quiet that a heavy snow brings. She slowly got out of bed and immediately grabbed her slippers. Reaching into the back of the closet, she pulled out her well-worn, old, fleece-lined flannel shirt that Charley had bought her for Christmas nearly a decade ago. It was her favorite shirt and it made her feel warm and comfortable. Opening the curtains, her eyes lit up at the sight of complete white outside. There were still huge snowflakes falling from the bright sky, but it looked like it could quit at any time. Walking to the middle of the window, she stood in front of it taking in all of the changes from yesterday. Immediately she noticed that her sidewalk had been shoveled. Glancing at the wall clock, she tried to imagine who might have done that for her so early in the morning. She felt the coolness coming off the glass.

The truck that had woken her up in the middle of her dream last night was still sitting awkwardly across the street. Tilting her head slightly to the side to analyze it a little closer, she observed that the truck was missing its front bumper and the passenger side headlight was smashed to the point that it was missing half of its glass. The truck was covered in a thick layer of snow which indicated that most of the snow had arrived after the truck had parked. It was also surrounded on the better part of three sides with a mound of piled snow from the plow. Making her now usual analysis of the upstairs window, she saw that a lot of the window was frosted over. She figured that was most likely from the crack. It must be freezing in there. Ada pulled her flannel shirt tighter together in the middle and crossed her arms in the hopes of relieving the sudden shivers that went through her.

Days like this used to be enjoyable. She and Charley would sit and make commentary about the beauty of the snow and tell stories about their memories of childhood snow events and talk about times outside with Joey growing up. He and his friends would make snow forts and dig holes to China and have snowball fights. She always wondered if kids in China say they are digging holes to America?

Joey would stay outside until he was practically frozen.

One of their favorite things to do all together was go for a walk after dark which in the early winter wasn't really so late. They would bundle up and walk the neighborhood laughing at who could blow the biggest burst of cold air with their warm breath. All of the houses would look snug and cozy with lights on and smoke rising from chimneys. After arriving home and shedding their layers of warmth, they would have hot chocolate or hot tea to warm their insides. It always made it especially enjoyable to snuggle into bed if you still had just a small touch of that chill from being outside deep in your bones. Ada felt grateful every night that she had a warm, comfortable place to lay her head. And she was also grateful that when she slid her cold feet over to Charley's side of the bed, he would move his feet closer to hers so she could warm them up. This was usually followed shortly after by him laughing quietly when she would warm up and then pop a leg out from under the covers because she was too hot. Ada smiled a melancholy smile at the memory. Days like this used to be enjoyable. Now they just seemed cold and lonely.

After her breakfast, Ada sat at the table concentrating at the blank sheet of lined paper in front of her. It used to take no time at all to fill it up with tasks, projects, grocery items or just things to write down so she didn't forget. Today she couldn't think of one thing to put on her list. Mindlessly tapping her pen on the table, she was glad for the interruption of the ringing phone. Should she answer it or let the machine get it so she could hear Charley's voice? She decided to answer it since it was a Saturday so it shouldn't be anyone selling something this early in the morning. She picked up right before the machine did. "Hello?"

"Aunt A, what do you think of the snow? Beautiful, isn't it?" Joe asked with cheerfulness.

"Good morning, Joey. It certainly is. I'm sure it won't last since it's so early this year."

"It will probably be t-shirt weather next week. But I'll enjoy this for a temporary tease of winter to come." He laughed but then got serious as he asked,

100

"How are you doing this morning? Did you sleep well?"

"Oh, not too bad, really." Ada stretched the truth. She never wanted to give Joey a reason to worry about her. "You weren't over her this morning to shovel, were you?" She asked still curious about the sidewalk clearing.

"No. I was planning to head over around lunch time."

"Well, when I woke up this morning, it was already finished and I have no idea who would have done it."

"Hmmm." Joe made the questioning noise in the back of his throat. "That's strange. Very nice but strange. I guess I'll have extra time to visit with you instead. I would call that a pleasant gift from a stranger."

"Yes. But you don't have to come today. You bring the groceries tomorrow. I know you must have plenty to do for yourself."

Joe wanted to check on his aunt's leg and to see if she was still feeling better. He had spent so much time worrying about getting her back to living and not shutting herself up in the dark all alone. But if she had seen that the sidewalk had been shoveled, she must have opened the front curtains again. That thought pleased him. "Well, I wanted to talk to you about something so I will swing by. I'll bring some lunch so you don't have to worry about what to make today."

Ada was already looking forward to his company but she said, "I can just make us some soup and grilled cheese."

"Now Aunt A, you should still be resting that leg. I bet some of that potato soup you like from the deli sounds like a good cold weather lunch. What do you say?"

With a slight chuckle and a large grin, Ada replied, "Well, that does sound delicious. Thank you, Joey. You're too good to me."

"Not possible. You deserve the world. I'll see you about 11:30. Does that sound all right?"

"Wonderful. I'll see you then." Ada once again had something to look forward to. After hanging up the phone, Ada wondered what it could be that Joey wanted to talk to her about. There was no use in guessing. She would just have to wait and see.

Looking back at her vacant list on the table, she decided to go sit and enjoy the lovely white landscape while she crocheted a bit more of the hat. She did grab the note pad and pen to set on the small end table by her chair just in case something came to her mind. There was nothing worse than having a great idea or thought but by the time you got up to get the pen and paper, you couldn't remember what the great idea or thought was. Now she felt prepared.

After a few more rows were completed on the small green hat, she glanced out the window as the mailman, Cliff, walked by the front of the house. He was walking in the road since most of the sidewalks hadn't been shoveled yet. He saw her in the window and nodded a greeting. He gestured with his bundled-up arm to her clear sidewalk and she could read his lips as he loudly stated, "Thank you!" A big puff of a misty cloud proved the cold air. Well, that and his bright red nose and glistening, shiny eyes. As he was halfway up the walk to her house with several envelopes already in his hand, a feisty squirrel ran to the edge of a branch of the tree on one side of the walk and swung through the air across the several feet to the branch reaching towards it on the other side of the walk. Cliff glanced up to see what the commotion was all about. In the process of switching branches, the squirrel knocked a big clump of damp snow from off the limb of the tree and landed right onto Cliff's forehead. Ada gasped and covered her mouth with several fingers. She didn't know what her expression would look like. Cliff looked into the window and made eye contact with her. He reached up with his gloved hand that didn't hold the mail and swept most of the snow off his face. Then he leaned over a bit and shook his head back and forth to loosen the remaining snow. As he looked back up, there were cold, wet drops of water across his whole face. It was even redder than before. When they made eye contact again, Cliff could see the look of almost horror in Ada's face. He couldn't tell if it was horror at what happened or horror that she realized she really wanted to laugh. He pursed his lips together and then bust out laughing. Ada followed suit and soon they were both doubled over hardly able to catch their breath from the gales of laughter. Now Cliff's eyes were shiny because of laughter tears not cold air. He felt like a million bucks to be able to see her laugh again even if it was at his expense. Especially because it was at his expense. He, along with so many in the small town, were happy to see her curtains open again and were hoping to see her get out and about like she used to with Charley. They were always so fun to run into in town. They always had kind words and funny stories. He always admired the connection they seemed to have. They brought out the best in each other. Cliff made the rest of his journey up to the house and Ada could hear the mailbox door squeak open as he deposited the envelopes inside. He had a bit more of a spring in his step as he walked back down her sidewalk and away from her house. He turned and looked at her still laughing through the window. He gave her a big smile and wave before heading on his way. Chuckling out loud for the next several houses, he was certain he would be telling this story many times.

Enjoying the distraction of Cliff's encounter with the squirrel, Ada went back to her yarn and hook. After just a few stitches, she set them in her lap and looked out the window to see if there was any activity across the street. She noticed that Cliff hadn't delivered any mail there. What could possibly be going on with the boy? She couldn't concentrate. Feeling agitated and unsettled, Ada got up and started wandering around the house. Why had she ever opened her curtains? When they were closed, she was sad but she didn't have to worry so much about outside events. After several laps pacing through the short path of the tiny house, she stopped and looked out the window again. She sucked in a deep breath through her nose and held it. Slowly she let it escape through her pursed lips. She imagined what Charley would say if he were here. Starting to feel a bit calmer, she spoke out loud to herself. "Ok Ada. The past few days have shown you life again. Everyone has gone on with their lives around you. You can choose to stay stuck in this dark place or you can look at the good things that surround you. Look at the beautiful snow. You met a lovely new friend who brought you yarn and her time and company. You witnessed Cliff get snowed by a squirrel." At that she couldn't help but smile. She continued, "You have a wonderful nephew that takes care of you. You have a warm, comfortable home and plenty to eat. You get to see the school kids every morning and afternoon. And there is a little boy who may show up across the street and might need to see your face through the window just to know he is not alone. You can't control everything. Just do the best you can. Every day." After her little self-pep talk, she cheered up a bit.

Heading into the kitchen, she figured the least she could do was make a pitcher of sweet tea for lunch. As she began thinking about that potato soup soon to be delivered by Joey along with a nice visit, she felt lighter and reached over to turn on the radio. It was playing an old Ray Price song. She and Charley would dance to this song in the kitchen. Their socks gliding over the worn linoleum floors. Charley would sing in her ear and Ada would rest her head against the side of his jaw. In her mind, they looked perfect swaying to the song. They had slowed down in their ability to move as freely as they wanted to, but they always felt extra close when they danced.

Ada was still humming along with the radio and puttering around in the kitchen with an occasional walk to the window to check on outside activity. She heard Joe drive up so she met him at the front door. He usually came through the back but it hadn't been cleared of snow yet. She took the bag of delicious smelling lunch while he untied his boots. "It sure feels cozy in here." Joe said as he made his way in stocking feet to the kitchen.

Taking the soup containers out of the bag and setting them on the table, Ada replied, "Yes. I had to tip up the heat a degree or two this morning. It was just a bit too drafty."

"That was a good call Aunt A." He said jovially with a peck on her cheek and quick fever check. "How are you feeling?"

"Oh, right as rain. Back to normal I expect, so no need to fuss anymore," she stated.

Joe gave her a teasing shocked face. "Well, if I didn't fuss over you what would I do with all my time?"

With light-hearted banter, she answered, "Joey, really? Sarcasm doesn't look good on you."

Holding a hand up to cover his hurt heart, he replied, "Not true. I carry it quite well. It's my favorite form of wit. If I lost that, I wouldn't have much to work with."

Each taking their place at the table, Joe looked at her and tilted his head. "Did you cut your hair?"

Putting one hand up to fluff the tips a bit, Ada replied, "Rebecca did."

With a nod and a smile that held a little more character than usual, he complimented, "It looks really nice."

"Thank you. I think so too." Taking a tiny bite of soup off the edge of a spoon in the hopes of not burning her tongue, Ada made a complimentary noise of approval.

"They do know how to make a good soup, don't they?" Joe said as he opened a pack of crackers to dip in the thick mixture. "Do you think it would be as good without the cheese and bacon on top?"

Ada shook her head instantly. "Bacon makes everything better. It wouldn't be the same without it."

"Agree."

After several more bites of the hot soup, Ada asked, "What did you want to talk to me about?"

"Oh! Right." Joe reached up and scratched the back of his head then brought his hand down and ran it several times across his jaw with its one-day old beard growth. "Umm. Well. Ok."

Ada could feel her forehead crease as she raised her eyebrows. Joe was never nervous. What was this all about? "Joey. What's going on?" She was more curious than anything.

Rubbing his hands down his pants legs, he fidgeted and finally blurted out, "What would you say if I wanted to ask Rebecca out for dinner?"

"Rebecca, my home health nurse?"

He gave her a look and she held up her hand to stop him from speaking. "Remember what I said about sarcasm."

He smirked and replied, "Yes. Rebecca your home health nurse."

Trying not to give away her feeling of joy at the thought of Joey on a date with Rebecca, Ada began asking a series of questions. "What makes you want to ask me if it's all right?"

"I just want your opinion," he stated.

"I think she is a lovely gal. There is not one single thing I can think of that would tell me not to encourage you."

He nodded his agreement. "I mean it's just dinner. She might say no."

"Why would she say no? That would be crazy. Look at you. You are a well-respected member of the community, you are an excellent doctor, you are handsome."

Not one for taking compliments very well, he started getting uncomfortable. "Ok, Aunt A. That's fine."

She kept going, just to tease him a little more. "You have good manners. You are charming. You have a terrific aunt."

At this he laughed out loud. "Well, now it's getting a little deep in here."

"Joey. Honestly! I think it's a nice idea. She would be lucky for the chance of your company."

With a slight tinge of red on his neck, he tried to end the conversation by saying, "I think I will be the lucky one if she says yes."

"Well, that's adorable. That's what that is." Her mood sure had changed drastically since this morning when she had felt so gloomy. "When are you going to ask her?"

"I think she comes by the hospital to get her schedule for the week on Monday morning. I may ask her then."

"That sounds like a great plan. She has been so helpful to me. I'm glad you recommended having someone come in to help me. It has taken a while, but I feel like maybe I have finally turned a corner." Ada said, ending the sentence quietly and with a thoughtful look in her eyes. She hadn't realized it until now but that might be exactly what happened. She had started opening herself up by finally letting the sunshine back into her home. But allowing another person back into her life had made a huge difference in her outlook. Of course, it was helpful that the person had been so sweet and caring.

After their lunch, Joe stayed for a while to play cards and visit. He checked her leg and was impressed with how quickly it was healing. He told her, "I think you might have superpowers."

With a smile, she responded, "I think you might be right. I feel more powerful every day."

When Ada walked Joe to the door, they commented on how quickly the snow was melting. It was amazing what a few degrees and a little sunshine could accomplish. Joe made a comment on the rough-looking truck chaotically parked across the street.

Ada acknowledged the curb parked vehicle and asked, "Do you know anything about who lives there? I have seen a little boy several times but not in the past few days. He seemed very lonely when I saw him."

Joe shook his head. "I believe there are just renters in there for a while. They aren't causing you any trouble, are they?"

"Oh no. I was just curious." The air smelled damp and fresh with the rapidly melting snow. Water was running down the gutters and along the road edges looking for the storm drains. Ada stopped and took notice of the concrete statue at the bottom of the porch steps. It was a little girl holding a basket like it was full of something heavy. She and Charley had spotted it at a flea market many years ago. Ada had instantly fallen in love with that little girl. Charley would always comment when they walked past her, "She's working hard today." They would plant seasonal flowers in the basket so it appeared she was carrying the load of their choice pickings. Looking at it now, Ada felt unexpectedly sad at the empty basket.

Noticing the look on her face, Joe followed her gaze. He asked thoughtfully, "Aunt A, how about I pick up something to plant in there? Do you think some tiny mums or maybe a little stack of pumpkins?"

She reached over and pulled on his arm to bring his face down to her level so she could kiss him on the cheek. "You are a very kind person. I would like that. Whatever you find will be perfect. And Joey?" She patted him lightly on the cheek, "Thank you for never forcing me to get better faster."

He wrapped her in a big gentle embrace. "Your timing is your own. But I have to say that I'm very happy to see you squint a little in the bright sunshine. I don't think it shined quite the same without you." He walked down the sidewalk stopping for a minute to pet the white cat that had plopped down in front of him waiting to be given some attention. Joe looked back toward the house and saw his aunt watching him. He shrugged his shoulders as he stood back up.

Ada cracked open the door and called out, "That's Oliver."

Joe grinned and leaned down to pet the cat once more but Oliver was already bored with him so he swatted at his hand and took off across the wet grass to the neighbor's yard. Joe waved his good bye and was feeling light-hearted when he drove away.

Ada closed the door, locking it behind her. It had been a delightful afternoon. She realized that she was already missing Joe's company. Rebecca wouldn't be here until Monday. Was she actually starting to crave personal interaction? She had begun to wonder if she would ever want to be around people again.

Sitting down, she picked up her book and read several chapters. Reading wasn't the same without Charley's communication, but she figured she might as well get used to it. She still stopped after each chapter to think about what she read and tried to decipher who was the bad guy from the very beginning. Some people could be so crafty and sneaky.

After a while she started getting distracted which seemed to happen much more frequently all the time. She had been thinking about something since yesterday. Finally deciding to follow through with her thought, she went into the kitchen and picked up the phone. She hadn't forgotten any phone numbers. Her fingers almost instinctively knew what to do. She dialed the number and listened to it ring on the other end three times before being answered. "Hello?" the voice greeted.

Feeling hopeful and without a hint of hesitation in her voice, Ada said, "Cynthia, it's Ada. Would you be able to come for a cup of tea one afternoon next week?"

Ada could almost hear Cynthia's smile over the phone. "I would love that!" Ada pulled the long, coiled phone cord across the kitchen and pulled a chair out from the table. She sat down and they visited for over an hour. It was like there had never been a two-year lull in their daily chats.

That night Ada slept peacefully and woke feeling more rested than she had literally in years.

CHAPTER 10

The peaceful, rested feeling didn't last very long. Opening the curtains this morning brought a dark, gloomy sky. She didn't remember fall being quite this aggressive with weather. She had to turn lights on as she went from room to room. It wasn't long before the deep, rolling thunder started filling the air. She could feel it rumbling her insides.

Storms brought a mixture of emotions for Ada. They brought a bit of trepidation with the always present, nagging worry in the back of her mind. Try as she might to pretend it wasn't there or to try to convince herself that it was silly, there was always the worry. She had never been directly impacted by a severe storm so there was no hidden trauma or anything to explain it. It was just always there on the edge of her nerves waiting to be pushed a bit too far. Was it the worry of an inconvenience due to storm damage? The fear of someone getting hurt? The angst for those without shelter? She didn't know.

What Ada did know is that she wished she could focus instead on when she had been happy during storms. When Charley would talk about how much the grass needed the watering. How the strong winds were just cleaning the dead branches out of the trees. When the power went out and Charley would read aloud by flashlight or they would just tell stories over candlelight dinners of peanut butter and jelly sandwiches. Ada never worried too extremely when Charley was there. If she started pacing when the tornado sirens went off, he would not even laugh when she got her purse and put it into the bathtub with their shoes and pillows to cover their heads. He would wink at her and say, "It's always good to have a plan, Ada Grace." To which she always replied, "Along with a backup plan." And they would chuckle. She knew he was just humoring her, and she greatly appreciated it.

They would sit for hours in their chairs looking out the window at the cars driving slowly down the road and watching the leaves and occasional debris floating through the air to a destination far from their starting point. Today, Ada just sat in her chair staring out the same window and not feeling much at all. It was not tornado season, but she wondered if she would have gotten her purse and shoes to put it in the bathtub if the sirens went off. She didn't think so. She thought maybe she would just sit in her chair and wait it out.

As Ada sat in her chair, she had plenty of time to analyze the house across the street. She knew her neighbors had moved for a job promotion last year. Rather than sell the house, they decided to rent it for a year to make sure the promotion panned out as expected. With a critical eye on details, Ada started noticing how run down the house had become in the past two years. Had it started before the Wilson's had packed up their lives to move hundreds of miles away or had it just been since the tenants moved in? How did that crack happen in the upstairs dormer window? As she squinted into the dreary, cloud-filled sky to focus closer on that window, the thin sheer window covering slid up and away from the bottom corner. Ada watched with curiosity as a tiny head inched its way slowly up until she could just make out two tiny eyeballs. The eyes glanced down the road from one side to the other then finally came to a stop at her window. He looked into her living room through the storm's darkness. She figured he could see her since she had the lamp on by her chair. She smiled and waved. He started to lift his head higher into the window when all of a sudden, he drew back and the curtain fell crookedly out of place. Ada could not see through the sheer covering but she saw the shadow as it lunged toward where the boy had been. Sucking in her breath with the surprise of it, Ada sat without breathing while waiting for any sign of movement. After what felt like hours, with a pounding heart, Ada stood up from her chair and did what she did best. She started pacing. Pacing and worrying. She needed a plan. And a backup plan.

Ada couldn't peel herself away from the window. She had made her decision after pacing through several options. She knew better than to go over there, even if she had been up to leaving the house. That would not be a wise decision. She thought about calling Joey, but she didn't want to get him mixed up into something that could quickly get out of hand if what she had witnessed of this man's behavior was any indication of his temper. The decision she had settled on was to call the police. She didn't want to stick her nose where it didn't belong, but she was afraid that the boy might be in danger. She was about to walk into the kitchen to use the phone when she saw movement.

The boy was slowly making his way around the side of the house. His eyes darting around and his head on a constant swivel. Ada held her breath and felt like her heart had stopped. The small child looked right through the window directly into her eyes. She didn't hesitate for another second. Almost running to the front door, she opened it wide as his little legs carried him at surprising speed across the street and right into her arms. She pulled him into the house and shut the door behind them and locked it. Looking down at the boy, she noticed right away that he was hurt. He had a black eye and a large bruise covering most of the right side of his face. He was trembling so fiercely, it seemed as if he would rattle apart. Sliding down the wall, she sat on the floor and pulled him into her embrace.

Hearing a door slam from across the street, it was followed by loud yelling. Ada pulled the boy's head into her shoulder tilting it to the side so one ear was against her shoulder and the other she placed a firm hand over. She hoped it worked to block out the cursing tirade that followed. The sound of the squeaky truck door opening then slamming shut was followed by a heart-stopping silence. Ada nearly jumped out of her skin when a fist started smashing against her front door. "Send him out here you crazy old bag." She could hear his steps moving towards the window. Slapping his palm repeatedly against the glass, she feared it would shatter. The boy was clutching her like he was afraid for his life and Ada was quite certain that might be the case. She stroked his hair and put her finger up to her lips even though she was certain he wouldn't dare make a sound. They were huddled in the corner on the side of the door and she knew the man wouldn't be able to see them from any window in the house. There had been a time when Ada had admired the lovely tall glass windows along the sides of doors. She knew only fancy houses had such extravagances. The thought crossed her mind at this moment that she was so thankful her home didn't have that luxury.

Coming back to the door, the man opened the storm door and tried to turn the knob to enter. Luckily, she always locked the door behind her. He was pounding and yelling his vile language. One thing for sure that this person didn't know was that Ada had a ferociously protective streak in her. Charley used to say, "Ada Grace, you can go from a sparkler to a firecracker in an instant." Where Charley or Joey was concerned, she was like a bear with a cub. You didn't want to get in the middle of them. Feeling that ferocity rise, she held up her finger and motioned for the boy to stay still. She slipped him from her arms and stood up facing the door. The boy curled into a ball, squeezing his eyes shut and covered his head with his arms. It looked as if he was trying to make himself invisible. Ada felt a surge of rage coursing through her. Her eyes lit with fire. Her fists clenched at her sides. She hollered through the wood separation, "I'm not afraid of you. You may think I'm a fragile old lady but I'm not. I'm a tough old gal. If you come here again, you will be looking at the wrong end of a shotgun. And I can promise that it will not end well for you. Get off my property and do not ever step foot on it again."

Listening closely, she heard his mumbled curses followed by the truck door slamming shut and the engine roaring to life. The tires squealed on the dry parts of the pavement. Lowering herself back to the floor, she leaned back against the wall and pulled the boy into her lap. "Come here, Sweet Pea. You're safe. I've got you now," she murmured softly to him. His tears started falling and she gently rocked him side to side. Her heart was pounding so hard she wondered if she might be having a heart attack. Lifting her head a bit higher, she told herself, "No, you just are feeling something again." With a slightly crooked grin, she thought that Charley would have been mighty proud of her.

It wasn't very long before the sound of police sirens could be heard in the distance. Undoubtedly, one of the neighbors called about all the commotion. She could hear pounding on the door across the street. "Police. Open up." When no one answered the door, they walked over to Ada's house. The officer knocked more gently on her door. He called out, "Miss Ada. It's the police. Can you answer the door?"

Knowing they would not leave until they knew she was ok; she slid the boy off her lap again. His eyes were huge and pleading as they looked into hers. She winked at him and gave him a reassuring smile. Using a great deal of what little strength she had left, she once again lifted herself off the floor. Walking over to the window, she tapped on it to get the officer's attention. He walked over to talk to her through the barrier. Ada's breath caught when she realized that it was the same officer who had informed her of Charley's death.

With sympathetic eyes indicating that he definitely remembered their last encounter, he asked her, "Miss Ada, did you see anything going on across the street a short time ago?"

Shaking her head signaling a negative response, she hoped she didn't look as frazzled as she felt.

"Someone reported the gentleman across the street was bothering you."

Ada replied as calmly as she could, "He left. I think he just got confused. He was driving an old blue pickup truck with a gray door and no bumper."

"Ok. Thank you, ma'am. Is everything all right with you?" he asked politely.

Nodding, she smiled. "Thank you."

"Have a good day." The officer walked back down the sidewalk and headed over to the neighbor's house. Ada hoped that no one had seen the boy run over here. Directing her attention back to the boy, she headed back over and once again sat on the floor next to him. She was sure that one of these times she wouldn't be able to get back up. As soon as she was situated in her spot, he climbed back into her lap. Brushing the hair out of his face, she took a closer look at his bruised face. "What's your name, Sweet Pea?"

His eyes glanced around the room and back to her face several times before he quietly answered, "Owen."

She smiled welcomingly. "Hello, Owen. My name is Miss Ada." After several minutes of silence, Ada said, "It's nice to finally meet you, Owen." They sat in more silence. She had so many questions but didn't want to rush him. His stomach started grumbling. "Owen. How about if we make a plan? Do you like plans?"

Owen slightly nodded his head with some uncertainty.

"Well, if you had to make it through that doorway right there," Ada pointed in the direction of the kitchen. "But you wanted to stay low to the ground like a little baby shark swimming in shallow water," she made a gesture of sideways waves with her hand, "how do you think you would do that?"

Seeming to actually put some thought into it, several seconds went past before he replied in his timid voice, "I would crawl or roll."

With a big smile on her face, Ada exclaimed, "Those are both great answers, Owen! Which do you think would be more fun?"

Thinking for a bit longer, he answered, "Crawl. I might roll the wrong way."

Laughing quietly, Ada said, "How about if I meet you through that doorway?" Ada reached up and grabbed the door handle to help her once again get off the ground. She looked through the window to make sure there wasn't anyone nearby and said with enthusiasm, "On your mark, get set...GO!"

Owen started crawling toward the kitchen and Ada made her way in short order. She quickly went to the small kitchen window over the sink and closed the curtain along with the covering on the back door window. Pulling out a chair she waited for him to take a seat before pushing it back in slightly. She went to the refrigerator and grabbed the milk along with a glass from the cupboard. Pouring him a glass, she set it in front of him. Trying to quickly inventory her food on hand, she asked him, "Owen, do you like pancakes?"

You would have thought she asked him if he liked Christmas! Almost breathlessly, he answered, "Yes." She noticed his milk was already gone.

"Well, let's get started then. She got the mix, a bowl, a spoon, an egg, oil, and her measuring cups." Breaking the egg into the bowl she gave him the half cup measuring cup. Hold this while I fill it then you can dump it in." He leaned on the table and pulled himself into a kneeling position. His eyes were so big. She wondered if he had never done this before. It made her sad to think he may not have. She poured the oil in and nodded for him to dump it. He slowly tipped it and held it as he watched the final drops of oil dripping off the end of the measuring cup. Then she filled it with milk and he dumped it in. Grabbing the bigger cup, she filled it with pancake mix and he plopped it in. "Ok. Now you have to mix it with this spoon. Don't go too fast or it will go everywhere." He slowly started stirring until the items starting mixing.

She smiled at what she assumed was a concentration habit as he chewed on his tongue. He was staring at the mixture. Once in a while he lifted up the spoon to let the batter drip off. "Owen, do you think we should add a secret ingredient?" As if in awe, he ever so slightly nodded his head. Ada took the vanilla from the spice shelf and put a few drops in the bowl. Owen watched it swirl as he stirred it into the mix.

Letting the pan get hot on the burner, she took out the syrup and orange juice and some microwave bacon which she thought might be one of the greatest ideas anyone ever had. Quick and easy and no greasy mess to clean up. Looking over at Owen, she thought his mouth might be watering because he kept licking his lips. She tried not to think about how long it might have been since he last had food. He was pretty small. "How old are you, Owen?"

He held up four fingers.

Ada turned to pour the pancake batter into the pan. She nodded her head. "Four is a good age. You can do about anything at four, can't you?"

Owen nodded in agreement. "But I can't drive."

"Well, no. I suppose that's true." Ada said trying to hold back her laugh. She stood by the stove waiting for bubbles to appear on the surface of the batter. After flipping them, she turned on the microwave for the bacon and poured the orange juice. She set out the plates and forks. Ada was impressed with Owen's patience. He didn't once complain that it was taking too long or ask how much longer until it was ready. She wondered if it was because he had very good manners or if he was just afraid to speak. As she slid the pancake onto his plate, he sat with his eyes glued to the food. "Do you want me to pour your syrup for you?" Ada asked.

"Yes," he replied.

Making a puddle of dark syrup on the edge of his plate, she was shocked when he didn't pick up his fork and dive in. "Go ahead, Owen. Don't eat too fast or you might get a belly ache." She took the seat next to him.

Owen's eyes darted around the room and kept looking toward the back door and the living room.

Ada's sorrow was felt deep. She said quietly, "Look at me, Sweet Pea."

He turned his head and looked toward her but not into her eyes.

"Owen. Look at me."

His eyes slowly raised to look into her caring gaze. She noticed that he had started trembling ever so slightly.

"You're safe here. You can eat. I'm not going to let anything happen to you. Ok?" She smiled at him and he looked back down at his food. He nodded and reached for his fork. As he did, his sleeve slid up just enough to reveal a mark on his wrist. Trying not to gasp or show any recognition on her face, she was certain that it was burns from a rope or cord. Did that awful man have this sweet boy tied up in that cold upstairs room across the street? Why had she waited so long to do something? She started to feel sick. Ada decided then and there that she would do whatever it took to see that this child was never hurt again.

They both practically jumped off their seats when the phone's ring shrilled through the quiet kitchen. The only sound had been the clock ticking in the other room and Owen's fork scraping the plate as he now ate heartily. Looking at each other, Ada chuckled to ease the tension. She put her hand over her heart. "Well, that will keep the old ticker on high alert, won't it?" She didn't want to but with the events of the morning, she knew it was best to answer the call.

"Hello?" She spoke as pleasant as she could into the receiver.

"Aunt A, I'm glad you answered. I just heard about the police arresting the man who was living across the street from you. They said he was harassing you before he left."

"Joey, you know how people exaggerate stories. I'm sure he was just confused about where he was. I'm perfectly fine." She looked back at Owen still sitting like a frozen statue at the table. She winked at him and gestured back to his plate to keep eating.

"That's good. I was worried about you. I'll be over in a bit with your groceries. Do you need anything else while I'm out?" Joe asked with relief in his voice.

Thinking as quickly as possible, she said, "I've had more of an appetite lately. Do you think you could get a bit more fruit than usual and I've been wanting ice cream sandwiches. Maybe a few snacks that you think I would like. Anything is fine."

Joe was pleased with this request. "Absolutely, Aunt A. I'd be happy to. I'll see you in a few hours."

"Bye for now," said Ada as she hung up the phone.

Making a plan in her mind, she followed it up with a backup plan. "Did you get enough to eat, Owen?"

"Yes," he said with a satisfied look on his face.

"Ok dear. You take your dishes and put them over by the sink, ok?" She put the rest of the stuff away.

After cleaning the few dirty dishes, she took his hand and started to leave the kitchen. He held back and pulled on her arm. Fear started creeping across his face again. She knew she would have to go slow and explain as she went with this terrified little boy. "Owen, it's ok. I'm going to show you where you will be staying."

"Will you be with me?" he asked in a whisper.

"I will always be very close. I promise."

With a look of relief and a tiny nod, he let her lead the way down the short hallway. She pointed to a doorway on the right. "That's the bathroom if you need to use it." He nodded his head so she put her hand on his back and motioned him inside the door. "I will not close the door all the way and I will stay right here the whole time."

She closed the door to just a crack and waited in the hallway. She hummed a tune so he could hear her the whole time. As soon as the toilet flushed, he pulled the door open. She walked him back inside and turned the water on at the sink. "You should always wash your hands with soap when you are done." She squirted a drop of liquid soap into his hands after getting his hands wet. He just looked at her. How did a child this age not know how to wash his hands? She was afraid that this was just the beginning of seeing what he was used to. Or not used to. She showed him how to lather up and get between his fingers. He seemed to be enjoying himself and if she hadn't told him to rinse the suds off, he would probably have stayed there for an hour.

Across from the bathroom was a small bedroom. She flipped on the light switch since she kept the blinds closed all the time and it was rather dark. Leading him inside, she said, "This is my nephew, Joey's room."

He looked around the comfortable room with the twin bed, night stand, dresser, small desk and closet. There were little knickknacks placed around the room and several pictures on the walls. Tilting his head to the side, he asked Ada, "What is a nephew?"

Ada forgot about all the questions that little kids had. "Do you know what a brother is?" she asked.

Owen nodded his head.

"Do you have one?" Ada wondered out loud.

Owen shook his head with a slight frown.

"Well, my husband had a brother. His brother had a little boy and that little boy is my nephew. But he is a grown up now."

"He doesn't live here anymore?" Owen asked with curiosity.

"No. He hasn't lived here for a very long time," she answered. "But he will be coming over soon to bring us some food."

"He will send me back." Owen said with tears in his eyes. "Please let me stay! I'll be good. I'll be quiet. I promise!"

Sitting on the bed and pulling him into a hug, Ada said, "Owen, I will do everything I possibly can to make sure you never go back. Do you trust me?" She felt him nod his head against her shoulder. "Ok then. Let's see what we have around here. I kept some of Joey's favorite toys in the back of the closet. Let's see if I can find them." She got up and opened the closet door. The first thing she saw as she pulled the hanging clothes out of the way was Joey's favorite stuffed animal. Most kids liked bears or dogs. Joey's favorite animal had been a large stuffed owl. It had only one eye and half of its right foot was missing. Over the years, it had gotten pretty worn out. Occasionally it received a rip or tear. When that happened, Ada would let Joey get into her sewing kit to search out a needle and thread to sew it back up. In the future, he would often bring up the fact that stitching up his owl might have been the reason he became a doctor. Ada pulled the owl out of the closet and turned around to show Owen. He wasn't there. With slight panic in her voice, she called, "Owen?" Walking over to the bed she peeked around and saw him huddled between the bed and the night stand. She wouldn't have thought there was enough room for anything between the two. His knees were pulled up and his face was buried in his thighs. Glancing back to the closet, she knew what the problem was. "Owen, it's ok. Come on out. Sit with me."

He slinked out like he was in trouble. Keeping his eyes on the closet, he slowly crawled onto the bed.

"You don't have to be afraid of this closet. There is nobody in this house who will hurt you." She held up the stuffed owl. "This was Joey's favorite stuffed animal when he was growing up. He named him Lick because he liked the commercial on tv back then about an owl who was supposed to lick a lollipop to see how many licks it took to reach the tootsie roll inside. But you can name him something else if you want." She handed the owl to Owen.

He reached for it and set it on his lap. "How many licks did it take?"

"As I recall, it only took three because it tasted so good that he couldn't wait and he had to take a bite instead," she answered with a smile.

Owen nodded as if he understood that completely.

"Will you come with me when I see what else is in there?" Ada asked without any pressure.

He shook his head.

"Ok. Do you want me to check it out and see what I find? It will be like a treasure hunt. I'll bring out the treasure I discover."

To this suggestion, he agreed.

She moved a few things out of the way before reaching the box she knew contained Joey's things.

She slid it out of the closet and pulled it closer to the bed. Pulling one corner of the cardboard, it popped open the top of the large box, she watched Owen's face light up at the contents. Everything inside brought back memories for Ada. Joey used to play for hours with the items inside. "Go ahead, you can take out whatever you want."

Owen scooted off the bed and knelt down beside the box. He stared inside for several minutes taking inventory. Ada was waiting with patient anticipation as he made his choice. His first reach inside brought out a gallon size Ziplock bag of matchbox cars. There were cars, trucks, several tractors and even a bulldozer. At the bottom of the bag was a vehicle bigger than matchbox size. He held it up to get a closer look.

"You can open the bag and take them out," Ada said, astonished that he was being so careful. He seemed almost afraid to touch them. She reached over and popped the opening seal to reveal all the pieces. He reached down through the maze of tiny cars and trucks and grabbed hold of what had attracted his attention. He gently pulled out a small semi-truck. Setting the bag of assorted vehicles down on the ground next to him, he sat back and analyzed the truck. He turned it over and looked at the bottom. He opened the tiny cab doors and the back trailer door. He rolled it up and down his pants leg. As he continued to play with his choice pick, Ada reached back into the closet and pulled out a smaller box. This one was heavier and she popped open the top to reveal a bunch of books. There was everything from *The Frog and the Toad* to the *Hardy Boys*. Pulling out several to choose from, Ada showed them to Owen asking, "We have time for one story before Joey gets here. Do you want to pick one of these?"

He looked over each book as if it was the biggest decision of his life. He chose one about Corduroy the bear. The cover showing a picture of a teddy bear in green overalls. "If Joey comes, I will have to get up to go out to the kitchen. We can finish this later. You just stay in here. You will be able to hear my voice. I won't leave. I promise. You're safe here."

Owen nodded his head. They propped the pillows up against the headboard and leaned back to get comfortable. Ada began reading the story. She was just a few pages in when she noticed him getting heavier against her. His breathing slow and steady. Staring down at his face, it almost turned her stomach to look at the fresh, ugly signs of abuse. She set the book on the night stand and carefully removed herself from the bed. He didn't even stir. Poor boy was plumb worn out. She covered him with a throw that was at the bottom of the bed. Watching him for several minutes before leaving the room, she wondered if she had gotten into this way over her head. How was she supposed to take care of a child? Well, things have a way of working themselves out, she reminded herself. She did have to admit something though. It felt good to feel like she had a purpose again. Her purpose was to protect Owen and make sure no one ever hurt him again.

CHAPTER 11

Ada had just been in the kitchen for a few minutes before Joey came through the back door carrying several bags of groceries. He set them on the table and she quickly started unloading them and putting each item into its correct spot.

Trying to get some information out of him without sounding too inquisitive, Ada asked, "Anything new going on?"

"Not really. All that snow melting so fast followed by the rain caused some flooding over by that low spot west of the school."

"That's too bad." It wasn't the kind of information she was searching for.

Joe asked, "What have you been up to today?"

Feeling guilty, she tried to quickly change the subject. "Nothing really. Is the rain done for a while now?"

"I think so. It sounds like we are in store for some warmer weather with sun again."

Ada was still standing in the kitchen. Usually, she invited him to sit and stay a while or at least offer him something to drink. He felt like she was acting a little off. "How are you feeling Aunt A?"

"Oh, I'm just fine. No need to even check the leg. It looks great. I've already checked it."

Pulling out a chair and taking a seat hoping she would follow his lead, he asked, "You seem a bit," he hesitated, trying to find the right word, "tense."

"No. No. Just these storms. They always kind of worry me. Glad to hear they are done." She reassured him by pulling out a chair and taking a seat. She had to encourage him to leave. It was too soon for him to know about Owen. When Owen woke up, she didn't know how he would react or if he would even remember where he was.

"I know you don't like them. We should be good to go for a while now." He watched her face noticing that she didn't make her usual eye contact.

Deciding to just come out and ask, hoping for details, Ada asked, "So, they arrested that neighbor then?"

Joe knew she had been underplaying her feelings about it earlier when he spoke to her on the phone. That would explain her tension. "Yes. From what I heard; he won't be back here any time soon. He had all kinds of arrest warrants from Arizona. He will be extradited to face those charges. I don't know if he had anything illegal going on here. I know they will be searching that house when they get the go ahead from the judge to enter it."

"Hmmm. That's interesting. I guess you just never know. Anything else they are talking about?" Ada asked trying not to seem too curious.

"I don't think so. Do you want to play cards or something?" Joe asked cheerfully.

"No. I didn't sleep very well last night. I'm kind of tired." Ada felt bad for lying. She was far from tired.

Reaching over to feel her forehead, Joe looked concerned.

"Joey, don't be such a worry wart. I'm fine. Just tired which I'm allowed to feel seeing as how I'm an old lady and all."

He chuckled at her choice of words. "You're not old, Aunt A, you're classic."

"Funny." She smiled. Knowing it would make him uncomfortable and feeling mean for doing it anyway, she changed the subject by asking him, "Do you know where you are going to take Rebecca on your first date?"

She was right. It made him uncomfortable. "It's just dinner. Not really a date," he explained.

"How is that not a date? Isn't that exactly what asking someone to dinner is called?" She knew she was pushing his buttons.

"I call it a friendly visit over a meal. You're feisty today. I think you *are* feeling better." He leaned back in his chair feeling glad that she was finally coming out of her shell.

Trying not to be too obvious, she held a hand over her mouth to stifle a deep yawn. "Pardon me," she uttered.

Getting up from his seat, Joe waited for her to rise as well. "I'll help get you settled before I leave."

That backfired, she thought. "Joey, I'm not an invalid. I can take a catnap without any help." She tried to sound annoyed.

"Yes, you can. I apologize. Call me if you need anything." He leaned down and kissed her cheek and headed to the door. Once outside, he was halfway to his car when he realized that she hadn't said her usual, "Lock the door behind you." Stopping in his tracks, he turned to head back to the door when he heard the deadbolt lock click. She usually only locked the deadbolt before she went to bed for the night. Deciding he was worrying too much about nothing, he turned back and continued to his car. He had to quit overreacting to everything she did or didn't do. She was finally starting to open up again. He didn't want to do anything to jeopardize that.

Ada rushed into the bedroom to check on Owen. Her pulse started racing when he wasn't laying on the bed. She called out to him, "Owen, where did you go?"

A tiny head peeked out from behind the bed. "Did he leave?" asked the frightened voice.

"Yes, he left. But you don't have to be afraid of Joey. He's a good man. He would never hurt you," Ada said with reassurance.

"This is his room?" he asked.

"It used to be his room but he wouldn't mind one bit to share it. Or share his old toys either."

"What happened to Corduroy? Did they find him?" Owen asked.

Ada could tell he was already starting to feel more comfortable in front of her. "Let's find out. Do you remember where we left off?"

"Corduroy knocked over a lamp." Owen said before getting really quiet and still. "I did that once. But it wasn't my fault."

"I'm sure it wasn't." Ada said as she brushed his hair off his forehead and kissed the top of his head.

After finishing the book, Ada made a suggestion. "How about if I find something that you can wear and run you a bath? I think there might be a boat somewhere in that box that will float in the water."

He just stared at her without seeming to hear her. She went over to the box and dug around until she found the boat. Handing it over to him, she took his opposite hand and led him into the other bedroom. She rummaged in her bottom dresser drawer for several minutes before finally pulling out what she had in mind. "Now I know this won't fit but it will do until I get your clothes washed." It was an old flannel shirt someone had given her about 20 years ago and it had always been too small. She could never bring herself to get rid of it because she liked the black and red plaid pattern on it so much. It wasn't like what you would usually see. It was a pattern so tiny that you could hardly tell if it was black or red.

She ran warm water into the tub and set out a towel on the side. Giving him directions, she said, "Set your clothes right by this door opening and I will grab them and throw them in the wash. The laundry room is the door right next to this one so I will be right here. Use this bar of soap and rub it all over your skin then get water on the soapy parts to get the soap off. Like you did with your hands earlier. Ok?"

He nodded his head with hesitation although she could tell he understood what she said. "Let me get you a cup from the kitchen so you can get the shampoo out of your hair." She started out of the bathroom and he was right behind her. She had to remember that he didn't want her out of his sight. She grabbed a plastic cup from the cupboard and was heading back down the hallway when there was a knock on the door. They both froze in place. Not sure what to do, Ada just waited to see if there was another knock to follow or if the person would just go away. There was another knock then a muffled voice called out, "Ada, it's Cynthia. I'm leaving a bag out here for you. Call me if you need anything."

Ada walked to the opening of the living room. She looked down at Owen who was clutching her hand tightly. He looked up at her. "It's ok. She's my friend. I'm going to get the bag and come right back. Stay right here." Ada quickly went to the door, opened it, grabbed the bag, shut the door and bolted it. She hurried back to Owen and they made their way to the kitchen table. Setting the bag down, she opened it and her breath caught in her chest. She had too many thoughts going through her head all at once. She started pulling the items out one at a time. There were two pairs of pants, two shirts, pajamas, socks, underwear, individual boxes of assorted cereals, some granola bars, fruit snacks, a coloring book and crayons. Cynthia must have seen what transpired this morning. She certainly would have struggled with telling the police that she saw the boy run over here. It's a dear friend who will trust your decisions even when you aren't sure of them yourself. Trying to keep her emotions in check she held up the crayons. "Look what you got! That will be fun. And now you don't have to wear that old shirt." Grabbing the pajamas and the cup, she asked him, "Are you ready for that bath?"

Owen nodded and they walked the short distance to the bathroom. He went inside and she closed the door halfway. She could tell he wasn't moving. "How about if I tell you a story while you are in the tub?"

"Yes," he answered.

Ada started telling tales about how there once was a long-haired miniature dachshund who lived next door that would always escape and come over to the porch looking for Joey. She could hear Owen get into the water and splash around. Between parts of her story, she would ask questions. "Did you use the soap?"

"Yes."

"Does the boat float?"

"Yes."

Partway through her story, Owen called from the tub, "What was the dog's name?"

Ada didn't have to reach far back in her memory. She had spent a lot of time getting after that little troublemaker. "His name was Nosey."

She could hear Owen laugh. He said, "That's a funny name. Why did they call him that?"

"Well, dachshunds have really long noses plus he always had it where it didn't belong. It got him into trouble more than once. One time he stuck it where it didn't belong and he got bit by a snake. Right on the tip of his poor nose. Another time he got stung by a bee. And another time when his owners had him on a camping trip, he got nosey and he got stuck by a bunch of porcupine quills."

Owen was quiet for a minute. "It sounds like he was a bad dog."

"Oh goodness no! He was a wonderful dog. He was just too curious for his own good. Did you get your hair shampooed?"

"No."

"Do you want me to help you?" she asked him. She didn't want to invade his privacy.

"Yes."

She opened the door, walked over to the tub and sat on the edge. The water was so dirty it looked like muddy river water. "I'm going to run the water so I can rinse the shampoo with fresh water, ok?"

He nodded his agreement.

"Slide back so you aren't too close to the faucet because it will be cold for a minute." Since his hair was wet already, she squeezed some shampoo into her hand and started lathering it up. As she ran cups of clean water through his sudsy hair, he reached out to let the water run through his fingers. His arm had a bruise that looked like dark shadows of several fingers. Someone would have to grab hold of an arm way too hard to leave that kind of a mark. There was a newly healed scar on the back of his shoulder along with several cuts starting to scab over on the back of his neck. She felt tears forming in her eyes but didn't want him to notice so she quickly put a stop to them.

Obviously, she knew she had to let someone know about the abuse. Whoever had done this couldn't get away with it. But she would worry more about that tomorrow. Tonight, she just had to make him feel safe and comfortable. There was no telling when he last had a good night's sleep. Helping him out of the tub and into his pajamas, she asked him, "Do you want to color for a little while?"

"Yes," he stated with some excitement on his face.

As they left the bathroom, she headed for the kitchen table and got him situated. "You sit here and I'm going to go close the curtains. Ok?" She opened the box of fresh crayons. There was nothing quite like a new box of pointy, sharp crayons.

She hummed loudly so he could still hear her as she walked into the living room and over to the thick pull cord to close up for the night. As she was entering the room, she noticed several police cars parked outside and it appeared that every light was on at the house across the street. Quickly so she didn't seem to be taking too long, she inspected the window upstairs. She saw shadows and could only imagine what they might find. Humming louder, she tugged the cord and shut out the outside world for the night.

Owen was watching and waiting for her return and look relieved when she entered the room again. She smiled at him and went over to turn on the radio quietly. She asked, "Do you like sandwiches?"

"Yes."

"I have peanut butter and jelly or ham and cheese. Which sounds better?" Ada asked.

Owen shrugged his shoulders.

"Ok. I think we will have one of each and split them. How does that sound?"

"Good," he replied and went back to his coloring.

"What kind of picture did you find to color?" Ada asked while she started taking out what she would need from the refrigerator.

"It's a dog with a big chew toy." He held up the book to show her. "What other things did Nosey do?"

Ada filled him in on all sorts of adventures of Nosey including when he got into a bag of chocolate covered pretzels and ate the whole bag. She stated, "Well, you know, chocolate can make a dog really sick so they had to take him to the vet, but he ended up being ok. You would think he learned his lesson, but not long after that he got up on the table and ate a whole stick of butter." She laughed at the memory. The neighbors always had funny stories to tell and they appreciated when Joey would take Nosey for walks in the hopes of burning off some of his mischievousness. Setting down a variety of food in front of Owen, she was curious to see what he would reach for first. There were the sandwiches, pretzels, raw baby carrots, grapes, a sliced apple and a banana.

She took the seat next to him and reached over for half of the ham and cheese sandwich.

He looked over everything before picking up the other half of the ham and cheese sandwich. Taking a healthy-sized bite of it, his eyebrows raised which Ada took as a good sign.

She slid the plate with fruit and carrots closer to him along with the bowl of pretzels. She reached in for a few pretzels. He followed her lead and grabbed several. She could see that he was copying what she did so she took some carrots and crunched away while moving her head a little to the quiet music in the background. This continued until all of the food was gone. He ate everything she had put out.

"Did you get enough to eat, Owen?" Ada asked.

"Yes."

"Would you tell me if you were still hungry?" she asked looking at him closely.

He nodded slightly and replied, "I had enough."

"Good. You can always tell me if you want something more, ok?"

He nodded again.

"I am going to wash up these dishes then we will go sit in the living room for a while. Carry your plate and glass over to the counter by the sink." He did as he was told and in a matter of a few minutes they were done in the kitchen.

Ada walked down the hall to Joey's old room. She wondered how long it would be Owen's room? Reaching into the closet again, she pulled out an old parking garage for the small cars. If she remembered right, it wasn't for matchbox cars but the cars that went with it should be in the bag. Picking it up, she asked Owen if he would carry the bag of cars. He followed her back to the living room and she set the parking garage on the floor. He sat next to it and quietly inspected each car as he took it out of the bag and found a parking spot for it.

Ada watched with contentment as she picked up her crocheting and got to work with another row. Every time her mind would start worrying about what to do about their situation, she determinedly made herself quit thinking about it. "It will work itself out," she told herself.

After locating a spot in the now-crowded parking garage for all of the cars, Owen glanced at Ada. "What are you doing?" he asked with curiosity. He crawled the few feet over, knelt beside her, and watched the crochet hook grabbing the yarn and pulling it through the spot she just stuck it in. Standing up, he leaned in to get a closer look.

"This is called crocheting. You use yarn to make things," she answered.

"What kinds of things?"

"Well, this is going to be a hat for a baby." She wrapped the ends toward each other and made a small curvature motion over the top to indicate where the crown of the hat would eventually be.

"What baby?" he asked.

"I just make them and give them to someone who knows a baby that could use a hat."

"Babies need hats so they don't get cold," he stated as a matter of fact.

Smiling, Ada said, "They sure do. Especially when it gets cold like it did yesterday. Do you know any babies?" She tried to sound casual.

"I used to." Owen replied then crawled back over to his cars.

After a while, Ada set her crocheting down and asked, "Well, you like ham and cheese sandwiches and peanut butter and jelly sandwiches. Have you ever had an ice cream sandwich?"

"A sandwich made of ice cream?" he asked like it was too crazy of a thought.

"Let's put your cars away then we can check them out," she told him. She didn't know who was more excited. Owen to try one or herself to see him try one.

Putting the toys back into the closet, Ada noticed that Owen still wouldn't get close to the closet door. Tomorrow she would have to find a place to keep the toys outside of the closet. She didn't know about Owen, but she did know that she, for one, was completely exhausted. It had been the second most terrifying day of her life and she couldn't tell anyone about it. Until she decided what to do, she couldn't involve anyone else. For all she knew, she might be breaking the law keeping Owen here. But she was willing to take that chance.

As they walked into the kitchen, Owen took what was now considered "his seat" at the table. Ada reached into the freezer and retrieved two ice cream sandwiches. She filled Owen in on some tips. "Let me tell you a few things about ice cream sandwiches." He looked at her, giving her his full attention. She continued as she started tearing off the wrapper on her sandwich. "It seems like a good idea to keep part of the paper on the sandwich. Something to hold on to. It's not a good idea. It's a bad idea. The paper gets soggy and your hands get messy anyway so it's better to just plan on getting a little messy and rip off all the paper." He followed her example. She set her sandwich down and reached over to push his pajama sleeves up toward his elbows. Carrying on with her tips, she declared, "When you first start eating, it seems like it will always be a nice perfect sandwich." She took a bite and watched Owen's face as he took a big bite from the top corner. She had to give him credit. He wasn't shy about trying new things. His face lit up and his eyebrows went clear up past his bangs, disappearing in his freshly shampooed hair. "By halfway through eating it, the sandwich will start to melt a little and slide around and you always end up with one big bite of mostly ice cream or mostly chocolate. That last bite always involves shoving too much into your mouth which is usually bad manners but it's acceptable for ice cream sandwiches. It's all part of the experience." Sure enough, when they came close to finishing, they popped the last bites into their mouths and they both had gopher cheeks bulging with too much food.

As they sat licking the corners of their chocolate mouths, they compared messy fingers. "You just can't eat them without making a mess. Trust me. I've had years of experience and nothing works. Now you have a choice. You can lick off your fingers or just get up without touching anything to wash them. But either way you have to wash them. I prefer just washing them instead of licking them."

"Me too," Owen stated.

Ada helped him off the chair as best as she could with her own sticky fingers and they went to the sink to wash up. He stood on his tip toes to reach the stream of water. Ada squirted some soap into his hands and he immediately started building up suds. After drying their hands, Ada patted her stomach. "I don't know about you, but I'm full as a tick."

Owen patted his own stomach and agreed. "I'm full as a tick."

Ada chuckled as she wondered if he even understood what that expression meant.

Letting out a long, drawn-out yawn, Owen stretched his arms out to his sides then slumped a little as he finished.

"I'm tired, how about you?" Ada inquired.

"Yes." He nodded his agreement. His eyes looked heavy.

Ada asked quite seriously, "Were you thinking one story before bed, or two?"

"A book story or one of your telling stories?" he asked.

"Either one," she answered.

"One of both?" he asked with hope in his eyes.

"That can be arranged." Ada answered agreeably. "First, teeth need brushing. We probably have chocolate teeth. Show me." She bent down toward him and showed him her teeth. He grinned up at her and did the same thing, showing her his teeth.

"We do have chocolate teeth!" he said with surprise.

"We better brush extra-long today so we don't get cavities." She put a generous amount of the kid's toothpaste that Cynthia had included in her bag of goodies onto the brush. He looked a little hesitant so she put toothpaste on her own brush and with slight exaggeration, she slowly brushed so he could see how she did it. After a minute of brushing, they took turns spitting the used toothpaste into the sink. It was obvious they still had left over chocolate in their teeth. "Let's rinse our brushes and do that again. Just to make sure we get all the tough spots." They rinsed their brushes and this time Ada helped Owen. Fairly confident of a job pretty well done, Ada led the way to Owen's new bedroom.

The book box was still on the floor outside the closet door. Ada said, "Why don't you pick out the book and I'll get the covers all ready. She watched out of the corner of her eye as he stayed as far from the box as possible. He reached in and grabbed the book that was on the top. He ran the few steps to the bed and hopped up, bounding to the top and squirming down under the covers. He leaned over to the nightstand where Lick had been laying since earlier in the day and pulled the stuffed Owl onto the bed, holding him in his embrace. Ada picked up the book that he had dropped toward the bottom of the bed when he jumped in. It was the same book they had read earlier because it had just been placed on top after the first reading. "Are you sure you want *Corduroy* again?" He nodded his head. "Ok. Here we go." Ada started reading again. His eyes started getting heavier.

He was barely awake by the end of the story. With a sleepy voice and heavy lids, he reached up and placed his small hand on her cheek. "Thank you for saving me today, Miss Ada."

She reached down and softly brushed the hair out his face several times. "I think we saved each other, Sweet Pea."

"Will you tell me a story about Joey?" he asked between a yawn.

Ada quietly and slowly started telling him in full detail about days when it was really cold outside and Joey would stand at the window watching for the school bus down the street. As soon as he saw it coming, he would holler good bye and run to the bus stop before all of the kids had boarded. She told about his favorite classes and teachers. It wasn't long before he was softly snoring. He was absolutely exhausted. She rose from the bed, turned off the bedroom light, left the door open and turned on the bathroom light so if he woke up, maybe he wouldn't be as scared.

She didn't need a story read to her that night. She thought she might have fallen asleep before she even laid down. It was the first night in over two years that she didn't cry herself to sleep.

CHAPTER 12

Waking up to sunshine coming around the edges of the covered bedroom windows, Ada was surprised at several things. First, she was terribly sore. It had been a long time since she had done so much activity in one day. Second, she felt very rested. Seeing how bright it was, she obviously slept later than usual. And third, there was a small body lying next to her on the bed. She watched him sleep for a minute. She hadn't heard him or felt him come in last night. Wondering what time it had been, she hoped he hadn't been scared when he woke up. He was curled into a ball with his arms around his head. Even in his sleep it appeared he was trying to protect himself.

Dragging herself from the comfortable bed, she did something she wasn't used to. She headed straight to the kitchen to the cupboard with the medicine and took some acetaminophen. Knowing she needed to have a clear head today, she couldn't allow aches and pains to distract her. She quickly went to the living room to open the curtains but hardly even looked out the window. Making her way into the kitchen, she picked up the phone and dialed the number off of the card attached to the refrigerator with a magnet. She cancelled Rebecca's visit stating that she felt fine but had heard rumors about the flu going around so she didn't want to risk exposing herself to it. Pulling clothes from her dresser, she quickly changed and went through a shortened version of her morning wash up in the bathroom. Before going back to the kitchen, she peeked into her bedroom to check on Owen. He was starting to stir and she walked into the bedroom and sat on the bed. His eyes opened slowly and she watched him scan the room and finally rest his eyes on her. "Good morning," Ada said cheerfully. "How did you sleep?"

"Good," he answered as he crawled out from underneath the blanket that he had brought from Joey's room to cover himself with during the night. He plopped back down on the bed and stretched from the tips of his toes to the tips of his fingers that were stretched over his head.

Ada smiled at his long stretch. "That feels good, doesn't it? When you get to be my age, there is a fine line between stretching and pulling a muscle."

Not sure what that meant, Owen asked, "How old are you, Miss Ada?"

"Well, I will tell you how old I am but just so you know for the future, it's not polite to ask a lady how old she is. Unless maybe she is under ten. But I'm 82." She answered his question as she got up from the edge of the bed.

"Is that a lot?" Owen asked.

"Well, I will count up to it later to show you but it would take too long right now. I don't know about you, but I'm hungry for breakfast."

"Me too," Owen said comfortably.

"Can you pick out the clothes you want to wear today and get dressed by yourself?"

"Yes."

"Then brush your teeth and I'll meet you in the kitchen. I'll start breakfast," Ada said.

"We brushed my teeth last night," Owen reminded her.

"It's always best to brush when you wake up and when you go to bed. Both. That way your teeth will last longer."

"Ok," Owen agreed.

Ada went immediately to the radio when she got to the kitchen and turned it up loud enough for Owen to hear it from the bathroom. She thought it might make him feel more comfortable and remind him that she was right here. She started singing out loud to Willie Nelson and found it funny because she had never been one to sing out loud. She thought perhaps the expression 'can't carry a tune in a bucket' was invented after someone heard her sing out loud. But she didn't care because she was feeling so happy.

Whipping up some eggs into a nice scramble, she added cheese and poured the mixture into a hot pan on the stove. She was filling the orange juice glasses when Owen came into the room. "You wouldn't mind having bacon again today, would you?" Ada asked unnecessarily since she already pretty much knew what the answer would be.

"No."

"That's what I thought. That's just like me. I could eat bacon every day. But don't tell Joey that because he would probably say it wasn't good for me."

Owen said with a comical expression on his face, "I would eat bacon ten times a day."

Ada acted like she thought about it. "Yes. I believe I would too. But you also have to do what's good for you. So sometimes you have to make those tough decisions like not eating bacon ten times a day."

"How can bacon be bad when it tastes so good?" Owen asked seriously.

"Great question. I wish I knew the answer. It's something about too much salt. Not good for the old ticker."

"Yeah. The ticker," he said shaking his head with the bad news.

Ada asked, "Are you thinking jelly on your toast or just butter?"

Owen replied, "What are you thinking?"

"I'm thinking just butter," Ada answered while trying not to smile.

"Me too."

Ada asked, "Do you know what else I have been thinking?" When Owen shook his head, she continued. "I've been thinking that maybe we should take turns washing the dishes. That seems fair to me. What are your thoughts?"

After some pondering, Owen replied, "That seems fair. But what if I break one?"

"Are you planning to break one?" Ada asked with a questioning look.

"No."

"Then it would be an accident and we'll just have to deal with it," she stated with certainty.

Nodding his head, Owen acknowledged this information as making sense.

They enjoyed their breakfast while listening to music playing quietly in the background.

Once the table was cleared of the dirty dishes and Ada had pulled the kitchen chair over to the sink, the task of dish washing began. Ada knew it would be easier to just do it herself but she also knew that she wanted to teach Owen as much as possible in case he had to leave. She wouldn't allow herself to think about that right now. She tied her apron around him to keep some of the anticipated water from his clothes. Squirting a stream of dish soap into the running water, she saw his expression turn to a question.

"Why is the soap blue?" he asked.

"That's a secret that I can't tell you until you turn sixteen," she answered seriously.

"Is that when I drive?" Owen questioned.

"Yes." Ada nodded her head.

"Sixteen sounds hard. How far away is that?" he asked with concern.

"How high can you count?"

Owen looked at her like he didn't understand the question so she tried again. "You told me you are four. Can you count to four? Starting with one. Two." He just looked at her. Not really remembering what age Joey was when he learned certain things, she decided that this was something they could work on. She was letting him wash the dishes without much coaching and he was doing a really good job. "Can you repeat the numbers after me? One."

"One."

"Two."   And so it continued until they hit sixteen.

"That doesn't seem like many numbers until I drive," he said.

Reassuring him, she ruffled his hair. "Your brain is learning so much every day that by the time you are sixteen, you will know a whole bunch. I'm 82 and I'm still learning new things."

"You must know a lot," he said with big eyes. He looked over to the stove at the only thing left to wash.

"I must," Ada replied while going over to get the pan. Knowing it was cooled off, she placed it carefully into the soapy water. "I know I think you can get this pan clean. Make sure all the dried egg is off." She looked at him with confidence in her expression.

With determination, he got to work on the pan. Ada helped him rinse it off then she dried it and put it away. Brushing her hands together as if she were brushing off crumbs, she stated, "That's done."

He made the same gesture and stated, "That's done." He hopped off the chair and slid it back over to its spot at the table. Hearing the sound of the bus driving by, his reaction was to run to the window to see it. He stopped himself before he got to the living room. The look of disappointment on his face was heartbreaking.

Ada tried to cheer him up. "It won't be long until you are riding on a school bus."

She couldn't decipher his expression when he said, "Where will I be when I go to school?"

Not sure how to respond to his question, she quickly changed the subject. "What do you think will be your favorite thing to do in school?"

Thinking about it for what seemed like an extremely long time, he shrugged his shoulders. "I don't know. What is there to do in school?"

What followed was a deep conversation about reading, writing, math, music, art, recess, library books, and playing with other kids. Everything sounded very exciting to Owen. Ada asked him if he had spent much time around other children.

"No. Not that I can remember. Just my sister. But she was just a baby," Owen said with a slight frown.

Before Ada could even react to that startling news, the phone rang. Deciding that she better answer so no one would decide to drop by unannounced, she answered before the machine could pick up. It was Joe and he sounded worried.

"Aunt A, are you ok?" he asked.

"Of course, why?" Ada replied curtly hoping to get him off the phone so she could talk to Owen about his sister.

"Because I just saw Rebecca and she asked if you were ok because you cancelled your appointment with her."

"Oh. Well, yes. With that flu going around, I don't want to risk exposing myself to it. My leg is better than new and that's why she was coming over so there was no need. I'm sure someone else with a real problem could use her help more than me." She tried to sound convincing.

"It sounded like Rebecca was disappointed. I think she was looking forward to seeing you," Joe said.

"I'm sure she was plenty happy to see you. What did she say when she saw you at the hospital?" Ada was getting good at changing subjects.

"She was surprised. She didn't know I worked here," he said with a smile in his voice.

"Did you ask her out on a date?" Ada questioned.

"Wouldn't you like to know? If you would have let her come over as planned, you could have asked her yourself," he teased.

"Joseph. It's not nice to leave me in suspense. I have her number. I'll call her. Don't think I won't."

He laughed. "Oh, I know you will if you get curious enough. Do you need anything? I'll stop by after work."

Realizing he was as good at changing the subject as she was, she decided to let him off the hook. But she had to convince him not to come by the house. "I don't need a thing. No need to stop by. If anyone would be carrying that flu bug around, it would be you. I'll call you if I need anything. Otherwise, I'll just see you another day, ok?"

With a little concern about her change of course after finally opening up to people again, he decided not to push it. "Ok, Aunt A. I'll talk to you soon."

"Bye for now," Ada said and hung up the phone.

Turning her attention back to Owen, she wondered if she should approach the subject of his sister again. He seemed a little skittish after the phone call. "Is someone coming to take me away?" he asked quietly.

"No." She patted him on the shoulder and walked over to get her list making pad before sitting next to him again. Figuring it would distract him from his current worries, she asked him, "Do you know how to write your name?"

He shook his head with a look of embarrassment.

"Well, we can fix that in no time at all. Are you up for that?" she asked with enthusiasm.

"Really?" Owen asked with hopeful eyes. He watched her print out a large O-w-e-n across the paper before handing him the pencil.

"Try to just copy that." She spelled it as she pointed out the letters. She had no idea the proper way to teach a child to write letters, but she thought maybe anything was better than nothing. She was starting to feel the weight of responsibility for all of his needs feeling heavy. Watching him chewing his tongue in concentration eased her mind a little. He was already starting to feel more comfortable around her and she could tell he wasn't quite as jumpy as he had been yesterday. She couldn't let him down by making the wrong decisions about who to tell about his whereabouts. Finishing up the last letter of his name, he looked up at her with hesitation in his expression. She smiled at him and said, "Are you sure you haven't been practicing this? You did an amazing job!"

He beamed at the praise and it lit up his whole face. "Can I do another one?" he asked with excitement.

"Of course. You do as many as you like." She watched him and continued to give him encouragement as she began the excruciating mental task of deciding who to confide in. She felt like whatever she decided to do, she would be betraying Owen's trust.

Not being able to close the curtains made it difficult because it limited where they could go in the house. However, she knew at this point that closing them would raise concerns with the neighbors and she didn't want them to worry about her. They passed the time in the kitchen working on letters not only of Owen's name but also starting the alphabet. Ada was surprised at how quickly he caught on to everything she showed him. She was afraid that he had been not only starved for food but definitely of attention also. They made lunch together and washed up the dishes. Ada read aloud several stories and she had him tell her what he remembered from each page of the Corduroy book. At the sound of the afternoon bus going by, Owen lifted his head and all of his attention went to listening to it drive by. "Can I go see the kids?" he asked.

"That might not be a good idea today but soon you can, ok?" she answered. Knowing he would be disappointed, she tried to distract him with another book. After just a page he was engrossed in the new story.

After playing in his new room for most of the afternoon, they decided they were hungry enough to start supper. With joy in her heart, Ada almost burst when instead of following behind her, Owen practically skipped down the hall to the kitchen ahead of her. He was humming a tune she didn't recognize but it made her feel like he must be relaxed and comfortable.

Owen brought his cars into the kitchen to play on the floor while she made spaghetti and garlic bread for supper. He had used cans of vegetables and boxes of various food to make an obstacle course for his cars to drive through. Ada wondered if all kids just instinctively knew how to make cars sound like squealing tires around the corners? Watching him with happiness at seeing him behaving like just a regular kid without many cares, she also had concerns for his future. She made up her mind that she would tell someone tomorrow. But she would do her best to make sure he could stay here with her for as long as possible.

The spaghetti was a big hit and Ada had to wonder where he put it all. He wasn't nearly as skittish as he had been during his first meal here. When they finished eating, Owen got up from the table and carried his plate and glass to the sink. Ada smiled at his cooperativeness. He asked, "Can I wash again tonight?"

"Absolutely. Thank you for offering," Ada replied.

"It seems fair," he quoted from the prior day. She chuckled as he pulled the chair over.

Ada had just put the last clean dish away in the cupboard when there was a noise at the back door. They both froze. A knock made them look at each other and Owen's face filled with fear. "Aunt A. Why is the deadbolt locked? I can't get in." She heard Joe messing with his key as he hollered through the barrier.

Quickly shoving the cans and boxes into the nearest cupboard, Ada got rid of the obstacle course on the floor while Owen gathered up his cars. "Just a minute," Ada called back, already out of breath from feeling like she was being trapped in a corner. "I'll come and get you as soon as I can. It's just Joey and he's a good guy, remember? Don't be afraid," Ada whispered to Owen before he fled from the room.

Ada went to the door and unlocked the bolt. Opening the door, she saw Joe's worried face. "Aunt A. What took you so long? Are you ok? You look very pale." He led her over to the table and pulled out a chair for her to take a seat.

"Joey. Why are you here? I specifically told you I didn't want you to come over and expose me to that nasty flu." She was shaking slightly from the nervousness she felt from the unexpected visit.

"None of my patients today had any flu symptoms at all. I spent a lot of the day actually stuck in my office on phone calls and doing paperwork. It's a good thing I did come over because you don't look very well." He reached over to feel her forehead. "Why was the deadbolt locked?"

Pulling away from him, she said, "I'm fine. I already told you. I'm good. No need to fuss."

He slid the chair out next to hers and said, "Well, you don't look fine." As he sat down and slid his feet under the table, he kicked something. Ada turned even more pale as he reached down and picked up a small matchbox car that slid from its hiding place. He stared at it for a long time waiting for her to say something. He looked towards her but she wouldn't make eye contact. "Aunt A? What's this?"

Her wheels were spinning as her mind tried to come up with some sort of explanation but nothing came to her. She deflected the question by stating, "You aren't supposed to be here today." She clasped her hands together and started rubbing them into each other. He knew her nervous habit and watched her face closely. Getting fidgety, she reached up to touch her hair, then scratch the side of her neck, then rub her bottom lip, then stroke the base of her neckline before rubbing her hands together again.

Reaching over and embracing her hands in his, he kindly asked her, "Will you look at me?"

It took her almost a full minute before she raised her eyes to look into his. As she did, hers filled with tears.

"Aunt A, it's ok. Talk to me. What's going on?" Joe said with such compassion that her tears started flowing freely.

"You can't tell anyone. I don't know what to do yet but you can't tell anyone," Ada said with an edge of panic in her voice.

"Ok. Tell anyone what?" He asked slowly and with confusion.

"He's here. I saw him and he was scared and that awful man was going to hurt him so obviously I had to help him," she blurted out then she held her breath waiting for his response.

Joe's brows knit together as if trying to piece together what she had just said. He shook his head as if he didn't understand then like a lightbulb went off, his eyebrows shot up in surprise. "The boy? The missing boy? He's here?" He was stunned at the nod of confirmation. Trying to wrap his head around this information, he sat quietly for several minutes. "Aunt A, they're looking for him. We have to tell someone. They have search parties out for him."

Ada asked quietly, "What are they saying about him?"

"It's sketchy. The mom's boyfriend took him. They have been looking for both of them for months. Someone made an ID on him a few nights ago and the police have been closing in on him. But when they caught up with him, the boy wasn't with him." Joe reiterated what he remembered from the news he had heard earlier in the day.

With a little hope, Ada asked, "So the boy's mother is looking for him?"

Pursing his lips together as if not wanting to give out the information, he answered, "Well, not exactly."

"What's that supposed to mean?" Ada asked defensively.

"She's in jail," he replied.

"What?" she whispered as she glanced through the doorway leading down the hall to the bedrooms. "Why?"

Feeling guilty like he was just passing on gossip, he said, "I can't be sure. I didn't listen that closely. Something about child endangerment and that she may be responsible for the death of her baby."

The air left Ada's lungs. She put her head in her hands, her elbows on the table for support. "He said he used to have a sister." She felt herself wilting at the thoughts going through her head. "Joey, he has to stay here. He trusts me."

"I have to tell someone. There's no way I can't," he replied with seriousness.

"What will happen to him?" she asked even though she didn't want to know the answer.

"I expect they will put him in foster care until they see if he has any extended family who will take him."

"No. I will be his foster care. He's staying here with me. He's been through enough," she said firmly.

"Aunt A. They can't let just anyone say they will foster. There is a whole process you have to go through."

With fire in her eyes, she glared at him. "Joseph Andrew Eldon! I am not just anyone."

"That's not what I mean," Joe said apologetically. He was surprised at her spunk. He hadn't seen that in such a long time.

"No one's taking him," She stated again.

"Can I see him?" Joe asked.

She knew having Joe on her side was a positive thing. He had a good head on his shoulders and he wouldn't do anything to hurt her. Taking a deep breath and letting it out slowly, she nodded but held up her hand. "Let me go talk to him first."

"Of course," Joe said patiently.

CHAPTER 13

Ada felt like she had aged ten years in the past ten minutes. She struggled to get up from the table and Joe had to help her. All of the different ways to approach Owen were rushing through her mind almost causing her to feel dizzy. She had to handle this the right way or he would never trust her again. She didn't want to be added to his list of people who had let him down. Walking into Owen's room, she found him in his spot between the bed and night stand. She sat on the bed and called quietly to him. "Come up here with me, Sweet Pea."

From his hidden position, he said a muffled, "He's still here. Is he here to take me?"

"No. Come on up here so we can talk about it." Ada was trying to pull herself together to give him the most confidence she could muster even though she wasn't really feeling it.

He crept out of the tight spot and climbed up onto the bed. He didn't look at her. His head was hung so low that his chin was almost touching his chest. He was shivering like he was cold, but she knew he wasn't because it was plenty warm in the house. She held out her arms and he leaned into her, slowly inching his way into her embrace.

"Owen, Joey's not here to take you. Or to hurt you. Do you trust me?" Ada asked in a hushed voice.

Owen nodded his head slightly.

"He just wants to see you and talk with you. I'll be with you the whole time. Is that ok?" she asked.

He didn't respond. It was like he hadn't heard her.

"Owen. Do you remember seeing me for the first time when you were standing outside and you waved to me?"

He swallowed and whispered, "Yes."

"I was scared that day and not feeling very well but you made me feel better. Did you know that?" Ada asked him.

"Why were you scared?" he asked pulling away from her so he could look at her face.

"I was scared because I was trying to start living my life like normal again and it was hard for me.

I didn't really want to face regular life. But seeing you made me feel happy. And I want you to feel happy. I want you to have a regular, normal life. Not to be scared. Do you understand?"

He shrugged his shoulders.

"In order for things to be regular, we have to trust other people. That starts with Joey. And I trust Joey more than anyone else in the whole wide world. I promise you that I'm on your side and I'm going to protect you. Ok?" she asked with a determined voice.

"You promise?" he asked with huge eyes that begged for her to be telling the truth.

"Yes," she answered. She got up from the bed and reached her hand to his and together they started down the hall. What a difference a few hours can make! Could it be just hours ago that Owen had been practically skipping down this hall with hardly a care in his young world?

As they rounded the corner to the kitchen, Owen hesitated and pulled on Ada's arm. Joe was sitting at the table. To Owen, he looked huge and intimidating. Owen hid behind Ada and squeezed his eyes shut. He was grasping her hand so hard it was starting to almost hurt her.

Joe was used to dealing with children who were scared. Most patients this age were afraid of him. It was understandable since most were sick or injured when they saw him. From the look of Owen's bruised face, it was not a surprise that the boy would be nervous.

Ada gently pulled him along behind her over to the table and sat down. She reached over and helped him hop up onto her lap. He hid his face in her shoulder. She made the introductions. "Joey, this is Owen. Owen, this is..." She hesitated not sure what to call Joe.

His patients called him Doctor Joe, but he wasn't Owen's doctor. Mr. Eldon seemed too formal and intimidating. Aunt A was the only one to call him Joey, except for the few times he had spoken to Rebecca. She had seemed to pick up on that name. He said, "Joe. Owen, you can call me Joe. It's nice to meet you, Owen." He reached out to pat him on the back, but Owen tensed up at his touch and he seemed to melt right into Ada. He pulled back as far as he could. Feeling awful that he made the situation worse, Joe sat back in his chair. No wonder Aunt A didn't want to let this child go. Trying to lighten the mood, Joe moved the matchbox car back and forth on the tabletop. "I found this car under the table. It was one of my favorites." He moved the small black Charger back and forth. "I think it was the fastest car of all of them. Is it still the fastest?" he asked, hoping it would be enough to get the child to engage. Waiting patiently, Joe was rewarded when Owen slowly moved his face just enough to look at the car out of the corner of his eye. Turning back into Ada's shoulder, he nodded his agreement. "You know, Owen, I used to have a real car just like this one when I was in my 40's. It was the same color and everything. It sure did go fast. It went too fast a couple times," Joe said with a chuckle.

"What happened?" Owen asked from Ada's shoulder.

"Well, once I got what is called a warning. The police told me I was going too fast. And the next time I got a speeding ticket," Joe said.

"Joseph. Honestly!" Ada reprimanded him.

"Aunt A, that was ten years ago. I was careful, it just liked to go fast. Why do you think I had to sell it?" Joe could see that Owen was relaxing his posture a little. He wasn't so stiff. He tried to keep up a conversation so Owen could get used to his voice. "Did you hear that it's supposed to snow again the end of the week?"

"No. It's so early for snow. The leaves haven't really even started changing yet," Ada replied. She watched Joe looking Owen over. She couldn't help but see the look of sadness in his eyes. To keep up the conversation, she asked Joe, "We had the ice cream sandwiches you brought over the other day. They were good, weren't they Owen?"

Pulling his head slightly away from her shoulder, he replied, "Yes. They made us full as a tick."

Ada and Joe both chuckled.

Owen was starting to feel more comfortable and looked across the table to where Joe was sliding the car back and forth between his big hands. Joe slid the car across the table and it stopped just in front of

Owen. He reached out and grabbed it, pulling it to his chest and holding it tight.

Ada said, "Owen has made friends with Lick."

Owen looked over at Joe to see how he felt about that. "I haven't seen Lick in ages. How's he doing?" Joe asked.

Owen nodded. "He's good."

"One thing about Lick, he is the best at keeping secrets. You can tell him anything and he won't tell anyone. He hasn't mentioned any of the secrets I told him, has he?" Joe asked seriously.

"No." Owen shook his head in defense of the stuffed owl.

"Good. They were just between us," Joe stated.

Ada recommended, "We should have some dessert. Joe, would you like to join us?"

"Have you ever known me to say no to dessert?" Joe asked.

"No, I don't think so. How does pudding sound? With graham crackers and a touch of cool whip." Ada slid Owen off her lap so she could start getting the food. "Owen, will you get three spoons out of the silverware drawer? One for each of us." She requested.

With the distraction of a task to be done, Owen forgot to be nervous. To keep up the distraction, Ada mentioned, "Joey, I was telling Owen some of your Nosey stories."

"Nosey was a great dog. Do you know what my Uncle Charley used to say about him?" He looked at Owen who shook his head and listened to him with curiosity for the answer. "He said he was two dogs long and a half a dog high." Joe laughed, Owen looked confused and Ada looked sad. So much for lightening the mood, he thought to himself. Joe reached into his back pocket and pulled out his phone to do a search for a picture of a long-haired miniature dachshund. Laughing when he found one, he said, "This looks just like Nosey." He turned the phone around to show Owen. "See how short his little legs are? He's half as tall as a regular size dog. And look how long he is. But he could sure run fast. It was so funny to watch because his back legs would run just a little faster than his front legs so it looked like he was running sideways."

Owen was smiling as he tried to imagine how a dog would look running sideways. "Do you have a dog?" he asked Joe.

"No. I would like to someday, but right now it seems like I work a lot so it doesn't seem fair to have a dog and not be home very much. Have you ever had a dog?" he asked Owen.

"No," Owen answered then stayed quiet.

They ate their pudding in silence, washing it down with a glass of milk.

After cleaning up their small number of dishes, they resumed their places at the table. This time Owen sitting in his own chair. Joe proceeded with caution knowing Owen might shut him out at any time. He looked at his aunt for approval. "May I speak freely?" he asked her.

She nodded her agreement.

Joe looked right into Owen's eyes. "Owen. The man who was with you, who wasn't very nice to you, the police found him. He can't hurt you again."

Owen was quiet and his eyes darted around a little bit. It was like Joe could almost see all the things going through his mind. "No. He said he would always find me."

Joe could feel Ada's tension. Joe replied, "Sometimes when people are being really mean, they say things to make themselves seem scary. They kind of like making you feel afraid. But he is with people now who will make sure he stays away from you. He is in a place where he can't leave so he can't hurt anyone else. He will be there for a really long time so you don't have to worry about him hurting you again."

"Will he be there until I'm sixteen?" Owen asked cautiously.

"He'll be there a lot longer than that," Joe stated.

"Longer than when I'm sixteen?" Owen asked with surprise.

"A lot longer," Joe said.

Owen nodded as he tried to process the information.

Joe asked with concern of refusal, "Owen, I have a question for you."

Owen just looked at him.

"I can see on your face where he hurt you." Joe watched Owen reach up to the side of his face. "Can you show me where else he hurt you?"

"This week?" Owen asked without flinching.

Ada could hardly stand it. She wanted to get up and leave the room.

Joe was surprised when Owen slid off his chair and walked over in front of him. He pulled up his sleeves and showed him the bruises on his arm and wrists then turned around and tilted his head to show him the scab on the back of his neck.

"Thanks O." Joe said. "Anything on your legs or stomach?"

Owen smiled approvingly at the name O. "Not now."

"Ok." Joe said.

With wide open eyes, Owen looked Joe directly in the eyes. "Are you going to make me leave?"

Joe felt his heart break. "I'm going to do everything I can to help you stay. You will probably have to talk to more people like you did with me. But Aunt A can be with you. Ok?"

"Ok Joe." Owen said trustingly. "Since I'm not hiding anymore, do you think I could see the kids tomorrow?"

"Kids?" Joe asked.

Ada answered, "The kids getting on and off the bus."

"Well, that would be just fine." Joe said.

Owen grinned and his eyes lit up with excitement. He put his small hands on top of his head and exclaimed, "I can't wait for tomorrow!"

Joe got up to leave. He had some things to work out. He looked at his worn-out aunt and was surprised to see life in her eyes again. She said, "Joey, make it happen. For me, ok?"

He hugged her and said, "I'll do my best."

Lowering his hand expecting Owen to "give him five", he was delighted when Owen reached over and instead of smacking his hand in a "five", he put his small hand in Joe's and shook it with surprising firmness.

As Joe was walking out the door, Ada called from across the room, "Don't forget to lock the door behind you."

Turning the lock on the door knob, he grinned as he called back, "Yes, ma'am."

After Joe left, Ada and Owen were both almost ready to call it a night. Owen headed right into the bathroom and started brushing his teeth without even being told. He put his pajamas on and climbed under the covers looking around the bedroom at what he already considered his home. As Ada walked into the room, she could see him whispering into Lick's ear. She wondered what he was confiding in his new friend. She could only imagine the stories that owl would hear. "What kind of story are you thinking for tonight?" she asked quietly.

He picked a Berenstain Bears book. She was happy with his choice since they brought back so many good memories. She was sure she had read each of them to Joey hundreds of times. After finishing the last page, she looked down at his droopy eyelids. "What next?" she asked thinking he would ask for a Joey or Nosey story.

She was surprised when he asked, "Will you count to 82 for me?"

With a little humor, she replied, "Well, you better get comfortable because this will take a while."

Smiling a sleepy smile at her, he wiggled a little deeper into the blankets and pulled Lick a little closer, using him as a pillow. He let out a long, deep, contented sigh which melted her heart.

Going slow and in barely above a whisper, she began, "One, two, three..." By thirty-seven he was sleeping soundly. Feeling like she better head to bed herself, she knew she wouldn't make it counting to eighty-two either. She hoped tomorrow would bring positive results and she did her best to not worry about it. Not worry too much anyway. Falling into a deep sleep quickly, she rested soundly until another vivid dream woke her up.

She was moving fast down an old dirt road. She wasn't running but she wasn't in a car either. Not having any control over her speed, she felt out of control. All of a sudden up ahead, she noticed a fork in the road. To the left was a cliff with a drop off after which she could only see sky. The right held a solid stone wall with no way around it. Straight ahead were woods as far as she could see with just a narrow path leading through a dense forest. Having to make up her mind in a split second, she chose the woods. She came upon the entrance to the maze quickly. Not having a chance to think about how to get through, she just focused on what was right in front of her. Eventually she slowed down and came to a stop. Turning in a complete circle, she looked all around her. The path was gone. She felt lost and scared. From a distance, she heard Charley's voice. "You're almost there, Ada Grace. You're doing great."

Starting to cry, Ada called out, "Charley! Come and help me, Charley! I'm lost. I can't find my way without you."

Charley's voice replied, "Trust yourself. You are so strong, Ada Grace. Find your way. I know you can."

Still crying, she kept turning in circles looking around at the mass of trees in every direction. Looking up, the thick trees blocked any sunlight from filtering through. It was dark, quiet and terrifying. Feeling herself getting panicky, she started drawing inward, not wanting to make the decision of which way to go. Looking down at her shoes, she felt helpless and hopeless. Wanting to give up, she felt herself getting weak and so tired. From behind her she heard other voices calling to her. "Miss A, thank you for saving my life." Owen's voice said. She turned around expecting to see him. There was nobody around but there was a narrow opening that appeared through the trees. The path had returned. Joe's voice said, "I'll see you after work. Maybe we can play some cards." Cynthia was in the distance saying, "I'll be over for tea. I can't wait to catch up. I have so much to tell you." Someone from church was talking about how many more babies needed hats before the really cold weather set in. The path was getting wider and she could see light in the

distance. The last voice she heard before waking up was
Charley's. "You've got this, Ada Grace."

She woke up slowly and peacefully. The morning light was just starting to peek its way around the edge of the drawn shade. Lying in bed and enjoying the comfortable feeling one has when first waking up, she let it envelope her for several minutes. Wouldn't it be nice, she thought, if you could get this comfortable feeling when you first get into bed at night? But instead, you fight getting your head comfortable on the pillow or are bothered by extra wrinkles in the sheets by your feet. You are too hot or too cold or have too many thoughts in your mind. As she lay there with her thoughts, she noticed that instead of them all running around in her head jumbling and crashing into each other, they were all coming together. She hadn't felt this clear-headed in quite some time. Sitting up and sliding out of the warm, comfortable bed, she felt optimistic that today would be a good day. She was ready for whatever it had in store. Maybe she would even add just a tad

more sugar to her coffee this morning as a special
treat.

CHAPTER 14

Ada walked quietly down the hallway as she hummed a tune in her head. She stood in the arched doorway between the kitchen and living room and stared at the curtains covering the front window. She could hear the wall clock ticking. It had been just over a week since she opened up her life again. Today, instead of being scared and hesitant, she felt confident and joyful as she pulled the cord to open the room to the early morning light. Not quite sure if it was going to shine brightly or hide among the clouds, the sun was taking its own sweet time to completely light up the sky. Hearing a slight thump sound, it was followed by footsteps running down the hallway and straight to the window.

"Have the kids come yet?" Owen asked with no hint of sleep in his voice.

With a light, care-free chuckle, Ada replied, "Not yet. We still have plenty of time."

Owen stood at the window looking out for the first time since being here. It was interesting to watch his face take it all in. She could see his eyes make their way to the upstairs window across the street. How many times had she wondered what was going on in there? She imagined that he would rather like to forget. He slowly moved his focus from the house across the street to the white cat sitting on the front step of Ada's porch. Knocking softly on the window, Owen grinned when the cat glanced over in their direction not wanting to appear too interested.

Ada informed him, "That's Oliver. I just named him. Do you think that name suits him?"

Nodding his consent, he said, "I remember seeing him. Is he your cat?"

"No. He's the neighborhood cat, I think. Everybody kind of watches out for him. I was thinking about making him a little place in the corner outside for him to stay warm this winter if he needs it. Maybe you can help me."

"Really? Ok! How are we going to do it?" Owen asked already excited to get started.

"Well, I think we'll start with breakfast and go from there. Why don't you go get dressed and brush your teeth while I make us something to eat. I'm thinking eggs and toast," Ada said.

"Just butter?" He asked seriously.

Looking at him with a heart full of love for this child who had entered her life so unexpectedly, she stated, "I'm thinking maybe we should try jam today."

"Ok!" he exclaimed as he ran down the hallway toward his room. He hollered from the doorway, "What about bacon?"

"We can't say no to bacon, can we?" she asked with a smile in her voice.

"No. I don't think we can," Owen replied while pulling his pajama shirt over his head.

Ada turned on the radio and started getting out the food. The song that was playing had been on several times over the past few days and she could hear Owen singing it from the bedroom. He got most of the words wrong but that made it even better.

In no time at all, they were done eating. The dishes were washed and they were sitting in the living room watching the morning come to life. Bruce drove by and slowed to a crawl to honk and wave. He didn't seem surprised to see a little boy in her window so she expected that the news was already around town. She had anticipated that as soon as Joey had talked to someone, the grape vine would move rapidly. Owen seemed to think that Bruce was honking and waving at him because he jumped out of his chair and went right up to the window to wave back with a big smile across his face. He swiveled around and pointed out at Bruce's car driving down the road. "Did you see that?" he asked.

"I did. That was a nice morning greeting, wasn't it? That probably means the kids won't be too long now," Ada informed him.

He stayed glued to the window as the kids slowly made their way to the bus stop. Some of them stopped and stared through the window at him. Ada could tell they were talking about him and wondering what he was doing there. She imagined it would be a topic of many conversations today. Several waved. Some pretended not to see him. Some just laughed. Owen was especially interested in the boys that as usual were chasing each other and seemed to be full of everlasting energy. Without taking his eyes off the activity, he asked her, "Do you think I'll have a friend like that some day?"

With certainty, she answered, "I think you'll have lots of friends like that."

Before he could think any more about it, he tensed up and focused all his attention on the bus coming down the road. "Do you think I'll ride that bus right there?" he asked as if it was the most important question he had ever asked before.

"Maybe."

She sure hoped his simple wishes would come true.

Ada enjoyed watching Owen take in all the activity outside. Before long the three high school boys walked by. Two were smacking each other and laughing as they looked in at Owen. Ada looked up in time to see the boy who she thought was the nice one looking in at Owen before making eye contact with her. He nodded his head once before quickly turning away. She almost felt as though he was giving her his nod of approval. That was strange, she thought. "Why are those big kids walking?" Owen asked, distracting her out of her thoughts.

"They live close enough to the high school to walk," she answered.

He made a sound in his throat. "I bet they wish they could ride the bus instead."

"Maybe," Ada said. She was once again distracted by a car driving up to the front of the house and parking. She immediately recognized the car and the driver. Why was Rebecca here? She got up from the chair to open the door for her. Calling down the sidewalk, Ada said, "I'm sorry you made a trip. Should I have called in again? My leg is fine."

Rebecca made her way up to the door and Ada stepped aside to let her into the house. Her smile was welcoming as usual and instantly made Ada feel comfortable. She realized that she had missed Rebecca's company. Rebecca said, "I wanted to stop by to visit if that's ok."

"Of course," Ada said as she turned to introduce Owen. She looked around the living room and realized that he had disappeared. "Do you know about the boy?" she asked.

"I do," Rebecca nodded.

"I need to go explain who you are. He probably thinks you're here to take him away. I'll be right back."

Walking into the bedroom, Ada already knew where to find him. Sure enough, he was in his hiding place. "Owen, come on out. That's Miss Rebecca. She was here for a few days to help me when I fell and hurt my leg. Do you want to come out to meet her? She's a really nice lady."

Owen shook his head which he had buried in his knees that were pulled up to his chest. "Owen, do you trust me?" Ada asked quietly.

He nodded into his knees.

"Ok then. I want you to come out with me to meet her. Will you do that with me?" Ada asked with encouragement.

Lifting his eyes to meet hers, he slowly got up from his cramped space by the bed. She could tell he didn't want to come out. She tried to encourage him by telling him, "Thank you for trusting me, Owen. I won't let anything happen to you." She reached her hand out and he put his tiny hand in hers allowing her to lead him down the hall. Once in the kitchen, Ada took the seat next to Rebecca and pulled Owen up onto her lap. He turned into her and wouldn't look at Rebecca.

To allow him time to get comfortable with her voice and presence, Rebecca just talked to Ada. They discussed the upcoming snow forecast for the weekend and Rebecca asked about how Ada's crocheting was coming along. Ada relayed her appreciation for the yarn which had allowed her to start up her hobby once again. Rebecca asked if Ada had started to read any of the library books yet. Ada stated that she was reading more about bears than anything else. She winked at Rebecca as she started talking about the bear lost in the department store who rode an elevator to the floor with mattresses. She shook her head and tapped her temple with the tip of her finger. "I just can't remember for the life of me what his name was. He's a cute little bear with overalls on."

She heard a muffled sound coming from her shoulder. Leaning down closer to his head, Ada asked, "What was that?"

Owen turned his head just enough to quietly call out, "Corduroy."

"Oh, yes, that's right. Corduroy. That is quite a good book," Ada stated.

Rebecca's voice was light and friendly as she recalled reading that story to her kids when they were young. "Corduroy found a new home with that nice girl who fixed the button on his overalls, right?" she asked Owen.

Owen nodded his head. "They became friends."

Rebecca wanted to keep encouraging him to interact with her. "I talked to Joey last night. He told me you were looking forward to seeing the kids at the bus stop this morning. Did you get to see them?"

His face lit up. "Yes. Right through that window." He pointed toward the living room. "Some of them waved at me. To say hi," he stated proudly.

Rebecca broached the subject nonchalantly. "I believe there is a story hour at the library on Wednesday mornings. There wouldn't be big kids like the ones on the bus but there would probably be kids your age. You would get to hear a few stories that might be exciting. Is that something you might be interested in?"

Owen's eyes got big as he looked up into Ada's face with a hopeful expression on his sweet face. Ada felt crushed as she looked over at Rebecca with a creased brow.

Rebecca had forgotten that Ada didn't leave the house. "I happen to have the morning off and I would love to go with you if that would be all right," Rebecca said, trying to recover the excitement.

Owen shook his head. "No. I don't think so."

Keeping the option open, Rebecca said, "Well, it's something to think about. Maybe next week."

Not wanting to let the opportunity pass since Owen had been starting to open up, Rebecca questioned, "I used to love playing Candy Land. Have you ever played that game?"

Owen shook his head, "No."

Ada piped up, "I believe we have it somewhere in the closet."

Rebecca asked, "How about if I went out and got us all pizza for lunch and came back so we could play a game of it?"

"Pizza?" Owen questioned with enthusiasm.

"Yes. Do you like pizza?" Rebecca asked.

"Yes."

"What kind is your favorite?"

Owen looked up at Ada, "What do you think?"

"I like every kind of pizza, except with artichokes. What do you think?" Ada responded.

"I don't know, really."

"Should I surprise you?" Rebecca asked.

"Ok." Owen and Ada answered together.

"That will be a nice treat," Ada said. "I don't remember the last time I had pizza."

"Me neither," Owen agreed.

"Well, that's a date," Rebecca stated as she got up from her chair. "Is there anything else you two need while I'm out? I'll plan to come back around noon if that works for you."

Owen piped up, "Is that a date like you and Joe?"

Ada held her fingers over her mouth to try to cover her smile. Rebecca turned slightly flushed and flustered.

Helping to let her off the hook, Ada saved her by replying, "No, I don't think we need anything. Thank you for offering. Let me give you money for the pizza."

"No, it's my treat," Rebecca said holding up her hand. "I'm looking forward to it." She headed to the front door. "See you soon."

Owen smiled and waved good bye.

Ada smiled and nodded as she hugged Owen close. After Rebecca left, Ada requested they go right away and make sure she was correct in thinking that Candy Land was somewhere in the closet. Owen was right behind her as she started moving stuff around the fully packed small space. "Aha!" she called out."

Owen scooted over so she could make her way back out of the crowded area. Setting the game on the bed, she opened the lid to make sure it had all the pieces. "What color do you want to be?" Ada held up the gingerbread pieces.

Not even giving it any thought, Owen picked the blue piece.

"Same one Joey always picked," Ada said.

Owen smiled and lifted his head a little higher as if he was proud to follow in Joe's footsteps.

They spent the time they had before Rebecca returned working on writing letters and coloring. Ada had just helped him bring his parking garage and cars to the floor in the living room when the phone rang. Owen continued to play while she went to the kitchen to answer the call. Always anticipating that it may be a call she wasn't interested in, she answered with skepticism.

"Aunt A, how's your morning going?" Joe asked.

"Good. I'm sure you know Rebecca stopped by to visit. That was a nice surprise. She's coming back over to bring pizza for lunch."

"That's nice. Look, I wanted to let you know that I've been in contact with the police and social services so everyone is on the same page about Owen. No one should be coming by without talking to me first. I'm working on a solution that will make everybody happy. How is he doing today?" Joe asked with concern.

Speaking quietly so Owen wouldn't overhear the conversation, she said, "He really seems to be opening up. He's more comfortable every day. Of course, he was very excited to have the curtains open to see the comings and goings outside, including the bus."

"Of course." Joe chuckled. "I have to get back to work but I just wanted to keep you updated with where we are right now."

"Thank you, Joey. I'm just trying not to think about it."

"Talk to you soon."

"Bye for now."

CHAPTER 15

Rebecca arrived with a delicious smelling pizza. Owen had helped set the table with plates and forks.

Ada asked Rebecca, "What would you like to drink?"

"Oh, just water please," Rebecca answered.

Ada got two glasses of water and one of milk for Owen. With everyone seated at the table, they opened the lid and the heat and scent rose to reach them. Owen leaned in and took a deep smell of the pizza with his eyes sparkling.

"We have half pepperoni and half sausage," Rebecca stated. "What do you want to start with?"

Owen looked over at Ada as if waiting for her to answer for him. "You pick," she said.

"Sausage, please," he said politely.

"Good choice," Rebecca replied as she slid a large piece onto his plate. She could tell he wanted to devour it but he was trying to use manners by using his fork to cut it. He was having trouble.

Rebecca cheerfully asked, "Pizza is so hard to eat with silverware. Does anyone mind if I just eat with my hands?"

"I agree with you," Ada said as she picked up the large piece and took a good-sized bite from the pointed tip. It was bent over her fingers and as she bit into it, warm, melted cheese pulled away from it. There were large strings of cheese from her mouth to the plate as she returned the pizza to the plate.

Owen watched her with surprise waiting to see her response. She just wrapped her finger around the cheese and pulled it until it broke then popped that part into her mouth too. It had been so long since she had enjoyed a slice of pizza that she almost felt like a kid again. She laughed out loud and waited to watch how Owen handled the cheese situation.

He lifted the slice up to his lips then at the last minute, he turned the piece so that he started with a big bite of crust.

"Interesting technique," Rebecca admitted. They didn't have too much of a conversation until the pizza was almost gone. Leaning back in her chair, she said, "You know food is good when no one talks."

"Indeed," Ada agreed.

After lunch was over, they played a not very competitive game of Candy Land. Rebecca and Ada were both surprised at how quickly Owen had learned to play. He was really happy when someone got a good card and felt sympathetic toward the person who had to go backwards. They were having a great time and Rebecca was just about to pick what they thought would be the winning card when the back door opened and Joe walked in.

"Hey there, everyone," he brightly stated. "Oh, I see I caught you in a game from the good old days." He walked over to kiss his aunt on the cheek and quickly feel her forehead. Pleased to see that Owen hadn't darted from the room, he said, "O, what color are you?" indicating the gingerbread pieces on the board.

Owen smiled at the new nickname and said a quiet, "Blue."

"Best color by far. Let me guess, Aunt A picked yellow?" he questioned Owen seriously.

Owen giggled as he nodded his head intensely like he was surprised that Joe had guessed right. "She always picked yellow even though she didn't win very often with it." He reached over to ruffle Owen's hair and Ada noticed him taking a half second longer to quickly feel his forehead for a temperature. It was the gesture he used on those he cared about. Ada felt her heart swell just a little bit. She just couldn't love him any more if he had been her very own.

Rebecca had noticed the sweet, protective gesture also. He made his way around the table and set his hand on her shoulder. "Nice to see you again, Rebecca. I understand you brought some pizza over for lunch. That was very nice of you."

Ada noticed the calm tension between the two. The best word she could think of to describe it was chemistry. It pleased her to witness it.

Rebecca said, "It was my pleasure. I have had a great day getting to know Owen and getting to visit with Ada again. And now, I'm about to win this game."

She picked up what she thought would be her last card and held it up victoriously when Owen's mouth opened up in surprise before he put his hand over it. She looked at the card and started laughing when she saw Princess Lolly. "That's what I get for being too confident," she said humbly. She moved her gingerbread piece backwards. "It's anyone's game now."

Joe took the empty seat at the table and was entertained by several more rounds of play before Owen won the game. He beamed and it lit up the whole room.

Ada smiled and teased him, "I'll get you next time."

Joe said, "See, it's the blue piece. I'm telling you. Stick with it."

Ada got up from the table as Rebecca and Owen put the game away. "Who wants some of Cynthia's cookies? She brought them over yesterday."

"You don't have to ask me twice," Joe said.

Ada got four glasses from the cupboard and handed them to Owen to set in each place as she retrieved the milk from the fridge. While she was closing the door, she heard Rebecca ask Joe, "Have you heard anything yet?"

"Yes. It's good to go," Joe answered.

Ada figured it might be something to do with the hospital so she didn't want to interfere by asking any questions. They all chatted while eating their snack. Once finished, Joe asked, "What time does that bus come by in the afternoon?"

Ada looked at the clock. "It should be any time now."

Joe looked at Owen. "Do you want to go watch for it in the living room? We'll be in there in a minute."

"Yes," Owen answered as he was already halfway to the other room.

Keeping their voices down, Joe began the conversation. "I've had word from social services."

Trying not to let her anxiety show, Ada casually replied, "Ok."

"They are requiring him to be placed in a certified foster home."

Ada shook her head, "No."

"Now just hold on a minute, I'm not done," Joe said. "That being said, this is the solution we have come to if you agree to it. Rebecca is certified because she took in a family member several years ago. Even though it was in another state, they have agreed to let her take him in. However, she will be at work during the day and it had been approved for Owen to spend the days here with you if you agree to that."

It took several minutes for all of that information to sink in. Ada couldn't imagine a better solution other than if he could just stay with her all the time. She nodded her head, "Wow. That's unbelievable."

Rebecca spoke up, "How do you think Owen will feel about that?"

"I guess we will just have to tell him and see."

"Give me a minute with him first, ok?" Joe asked.

Getting nods of approval from both Ada and Rebecca, he headed into the living room. "O, I have a question for you." Joe said to Owen who was glued to the window.

He didn't turn around but stated agreeable, "Ok."

"Do you want to go sit outside with me to wait for the bus? We can sit on the porch or the steps. What do you say?" Joe thought it would be an easy decision for Owen. He was surprised by his delayed response.

Ada and Rebecca walked into the living room just as Owen was turning around to head into the kitchen. He looked with hopeful eyes up to Ada. "Miss Ada, what are your thoughts about me going outside for just a little bit with Joe to watch for the bus?"

Ada almost teared up at the adorable look on his face. She could tell he didn't want to let her down with the wrong answer. "Well, I would think that you better hurry so you don't miss it. I'll be watching from in here too."

He quickly took several steps toward Joe. "My answer is yes. Please."

Rebecca and Ada stood at the window looking out as Joe and Owen stepped out the door and onto the porch. They watched as Joe asked Owen a few questions pointing to the steps and to the sidewalk. They saw Owen look at the steps then down the road in the direction the bus would come. Then he looked up and they could see just enough of his profile to tell that he was looking across the street at the house with the broken upstairs window. Conflict was in his posture. Owen craned his head down the street as the rumble of the bus coming could be felt before it could be heard. He looked up at Joe and reached for his hand as they walked down the sidewalk to the edge of the curb to watch the bus. Rebecca and Ada smiled at each other at the picture of new-found trust in front of them. Owen was waving as big as could be as the bus slowed down and crept by the two spectators. The bus driver opened his side window and reached his arm out to wave back at Owen. Joe turned around just enough to catch a good look through the window of his aunt and Rebecca. They were beaming. He winked at them and turned back around. The bus had stopped and the kids were slowly departing from the aisle, down the steps and into the street.

Most of the kids quickly separated in different directions. One young boy with untied shoelaces and messy hair didn't seem to be in as much of a hurry. He stopped in front of Joe and Owen. He said, "I saw you this morning. You new here?"

"Yes."

"What's your name?" the boy asked with curiosity.

"Owen. What's yours?" Owen held his breath wondering if his question would be answered.

"Well, my name's Johnson Smith but I go by Johnny," he said with complete seriousness. He was trying very hard to be mature.

Joe almost choked on a laugh.

Johnny looked up at Joe. "I know you." He held up his arm to show his elbow. "You gave me stitches right here." He pointed and tapped the scar on his elbow."

Joe nodded with complete composure and stated the fact, "Bike accident, if I recall correctly."

With a shrug Johnny said, "Yeah. I guess it was an accident. You know my brother? Well, you know how brothers are." He started walking back up the road heading for his home. Throwing his hand up in the air in a quick gesture, he called out, "See you tomorrow."

Joe looked down at Owen and thought the boy looked like he might explode. "Joe, he said 'See you tomorrow'. Do you think that means he might be my friend?"

"I think maybe so," Joe answered.

"I don't know what it's like to have a brother, do you?" Owen asked.

"No. I didn't have a brother or a sister."

"I had a sister but she and my mom left one day. But she was just a baby so she couldn't play or anything. I tried to play with her to stop her from crying, but it didn't always work. She was too little to understand that it's better to just stay quiet and out of the way."

Ada and Rebecca watched the serious conversation at the curb and wondered if Joe was telling Owen about the new arrangements. Rebecca relayed the information she had gotten earlier in the day. "If it's ok with you, Owen can stay here tonight and I'll pick him up after work, maybe around five tomorrow. Then I will drop him by in the mornings around eight."

Ada said, "The bus gets here about 7:50 so maybe you could come in for a cup of coffee when you drop him off?"

"That sounds perfect."

CHAPTER 16

Owen was a little hesitant with the idea at first but with the promise of coming back to Ada's house first thing in the morning in time for the bus along with being allowed to bring Lick with him, he cooperated without any trouble. He looked forward to seeing Johnny on his way to and from the bus. Owen would sit on the porch steps with Ada watching him from the window as he visited with his new friend.

Everyone had agreed to spend Saturday together. Ada awoke with such a sense of excitement. Joe had dropped off a quarter of a bushel of fall apples the day before and she was looking forward to making her special recipe of apple sauce along with some apple pie. She found herself wondering which one Owen would like better. So far, she hadn't come across anything he didn't like. It was streaming bright light around the corners of her bedroom shades. That could only mean one thing. She didn't even wait to let the light into the bedroom before quickly heading down the hallway to the living room. Even with slippers on, she felt the chill on her feet as she pulled the cord to reveal the glistening snow. It was magical! It reminded her of a snow globe. She was taking it all in when she noticed something on the side of the road. Leaning forward and squinting into the light, she could make out the form of a person laying on the ground off the curb across the street. She banged on the window. There was no movement. With her heart racing, she quickly made it to the door and opened it to yell outside. "Hey there! Are you all right?" She ran to the phone and called for an ambulance. She stared out the front door and willed the person to get up. The snow had started accumulating on the person so they must have been there for a while. They must be freezing, she thought. With her heart pounding in her chest as well as in her ears, she grabbed the blanket from the back of the chair and her coat from the hall closet and without letting herself think about it, she made her way out into the world for the first time in over two years.

She didn't hear any sirens in the distance yet. She was calling out to the still, snow-covered figure as she carefully made her way across the somewhat slippery road. Making it to the body, she brushed the snow off as quickly as possible and wrapped the blanket around their shoulder and neck. Still talking to the person, she reached out to brush the snow from their face and hair. Her breath caught in her chest as she immediately identified the freezing individual. Even though he had been beaten up, she recognized him as the boy who walked past her house on his way to school with the two hooligans. Not wanting to move him in any way in case he had injuries, she got as close to him as she could in order to give him some of her heat. She rubbed his arm gently and kept talking to him.

Still not moving yet, he groaned softly. "Oh, thank goodness you're awake," Ada said. "Come on. Wake up. There is help coming. You'll be warm shortly." She kept rubbing his arm and pushing his hair out of his face. "You're ok."

With a louder groan, he slowly opened his eyes with a grimace. She didn't know if it was from pain or from the sun against the brightness of the fresh snow. He mumbled, "You. Why? Outside. Help. Me."

She soothed him with her calming voice. "You're fine. I can hear the ambulance. It will just be a minute."

He sucked in a deep breath and started moving his body a little. As he tried to lift his head up, she encouraged him to stay still until the paramedics could check him over.

He seemed to have become more aware of his surroundings. He sighed loudly. Looking up into her face, he said slowly, "You're Charley's wife."

Her instinct was to pull back but she didn't. "Yes. Did you know Charley?"

"He saved me," he said staring out at the snow falling.

"He saved you?" Ada asked in surprise.

"I had gone to school but left after first period. I was walking home and had decided to do something bad to myself." He stopped to breathe a few times before slowly continuing. "I was just tired of struggling. He saw me and smiled. He looked like he was having trouble so I stopped to ask if he was all right. He looked me straight in the eyes and said, 'Right as rain. Every day is a gift. Enjoy them and use them wisely so you can look back on good times instead of bad choices. You have a lot of potential, son. I can see it.'" Tears started glossing over his freezing eyes. They became clearer in the cold air. He continued with a hoarse voice, "No one has ever called me son. Or looked me in the eyes."

Ada felt her cold tears. That sounded like her Charley. He was always being pleasant and encouraging.

"I went home and his voice played over and over in my mind. I was still considering ending it when I heard sirens. For some reason, I thought they were coming for me, so I ran outside and down this street. That's when I saw the ambulance in the road and the paramedic on the ground with Charley." His eyes filled with tears as several ran down his cheeks. The ambulance they had been waiting for was pulling up to Ada as she huddled over the boy. He grabbed her hand and held on to it. "He saved me. I couldn't follow through with my plan. I read about him in the paper afterwards. I'm very sorry for your loss."

The paramedic squatted down beside her, "Ma'am, let's get you warmed up. You're shivering."

By this time, several of the neighbors had made their way outside to see what was happening. Cynthia ran over from her house and helped Ada stand up. The paramedics told her to help Ada into her house and they would come to check on her there. Someone had notified Joe and he practically flew onto the street and slid to a stop behind the ambulance. Jumping out of his car, he was shocked at the sight before him. First, why was his aunt outside, especially when it was so icy and cold? Second, why was she so pale and blank looking? It seemed like she might be in shock. He practically carried her into her warm house and helped her sit in her chair. "Aunt A. Can you tell me what happened?"

She stared out the window. He asked Cynthia to get some water and grabbed as many blankets as he could find. With teeth chattering she smiled slightly and said with a scratchy voice, "Lucky these are my real teeth or I would have cracked them to pieces by now."

Feeling more confident after hearing her humor coming through, he knelt beside her as he gently rubbed his big hands up and down her arms to keep warming her up. Keeping up with her humor, he said, "Well, when you finally decide to go outside, you really do make a production out of it."

Lifting her hands from the bundles of blankets, she shooed him away. "Joey, I'm just fine. You go check on that young man. He gave me a gift today. One I could never have imagined. And then you let me know how he's doing. Please do that for me Joey."

The paramedic who had spoken to her outside knocked on the door. Joe went to open the door and they all agreed to him checking Ada's vitals while Joe went out to check on the boy. Cynthia came in from the kitchen with a cup of steaming tea and set it on the table between the chairs. After the paramedic left and Joey had given her an update on her new friend, she sat with her old friend, sipping tea without having to talk. Pulling her mound of blankets up and tucking them around her legs, she leaned back and sighed with contentment. What an amazing day. What a unique learning experience. She never realized just how many people are overlooked. People are living each day with memories, experiences and hopefully some good advice and wisdom from each of us. Ada figured it probably took numerous positive encouragements to replace the hurt of one hateful criticism. We possibly underestimate who we will touch with a kind word or patient response. Every single individual is craving love and acceptance. One never knows when a nice gesture or compliment might change someone's whole outlook for the day. Ada had determined that she was going to live her life again. She was going to follow Charley's lead and try to be the instigator of positivity. She could hardly wait to get started.

December 24

Today was happy and sad. Ada felt bursting with love and burdened with loss. Sixty-four years ago, Ada had married the love of a lifetime. They had led an extraordinary, ordinary life. Oh, how she wished Charley could be here to see all of the changes in the past several months.

Owen had adjusted swiftly to living with Rebecca. He came over every weekday morning and watched for the bus while Ada and Rebecca enjoyed a quick cup of hot coffee before Rebecca headed off to work. Tuesdays and Thursdays, Owen and Ada prepared a meal together for them to share when Rebecca came to pick him up. Joe would join them whenever possible. Ada could see a romance blooming between the two of them and she couldn't have been more pleased. She could tell by the way they looked at each other and by the way Joe would occasionally put his hand on her back when they were walking. Some people might not notice it but Ada could still feel the way Charley's hand felt on her back. It had made her feel safe and protected.

They all met for supper at Valentini's every Friday night. Owen had ordered cheese ravioli the first time there and was immediately hooked. He never even considered ordering anything else since. He was outgoing and polite with people he met. He walked with his head held high holding on to Rebecca or Joe's hand. It appeared that Owen would be able to stay long term with Rebecca since his mother had voluntarily terminated her parental rights knowing she would be in jail until after Owen was grown.

Ada still wasn't completely comfortable outside the security of her home, but she was getting more relaxed with each trip out the door. Snow was now a constant and it brought her some peace. Winter had always seemed to relax Ada. Daniel, the high school boy whose injuries had initially brought Ada from her house for the first time, still came by to shovel for her. He would come inside for some hot chocolate and a visit afterwards. They were becoming friends and he confided in Ada like he would a grandma. Owen was Daniel's biggest fan. He informed him every time he saw him, "I wish you were my big brother." It was a positive relationship for both boys.

Ada started listening more often to the records she and Charley used to play. She would picture in her mind dancing in the living room with Charley. But it didn't make her sad every time any longer. Sometimes it even made her smile. She recalled their teasing banter over the meaning of the words to some songs. Charley would say, "This is a cheating song, Ada Grace." To which she would reply, "Oh no. I don't think so. Let me hear it my way." She knew he was right, but she liked to rib him once in a while.

She thought her life was over when Charley died. She couldn't imagine ever being happy again. But here she was two years later with new relationships that brought her joy along with continued ones with those who had never left her side. She knew it would never be the same without him. It was a different kind of happy but at least it was still available in some form to her.

245

Joe and Ada had driven the short distance in the car. Arriving at their destination, Joe helped Ada out of the car. This trip was just for the two of them. Rebecca and Owen would come eventually. They had gone to the cemetery for Ada to place a poinsettia on Charley's grave. She had never been there before since she had been so frail with her illness right after his death. Looking around, she was pleased with the location they had chosen so many years ago when they made their arrangements. Joe helped her through the inches of snow on the ground. It was quiet as the snow buffered the sounds around them. Stooping down she gently brushed the snow off the top of the headstone. She placed the poinsettia on the ground next to it. The bright red contrasted with the stark white everywhere. It was beautiful. Hooking her arm around Joe's to give her some stability and comfort, he reached over and patted her hand in the crook of his arm. He said, "He was amazing."

Ada felt her eyes welling up with tears as she nodded her head. "He was extraordinarily perfect."

After several minutes of silence, they turned around and arm in arm walked slowly back to the car. Joe asked, "Is it ok if we go one more place before going home?"

Ada wanted to be alone after such an emotional event but she didn't have the heart to say so to Joe. She just said a quiet, "Alright."

Looking down at her lap deep in her thoughts for the drive, she hadn't paid attention to where they were going. It was about ten minutes later when the car started slowing down. She looked up to see where it was that Joe had wanted to go. Her breath caught and she turned to face him. He looked at her with anticipation and asked, "It's not too far for you to walk, is it?"

Not able to speak, she shook her head and reached to open her car door. Joe grabbed a blanket from the back seat and came to help her out of the passenger seat. They walked carefully and without words along a well-worn trail through the woods. Right before they arrived at the opening near the end of the trail, Joe stopped and turned to Ada. He was trying not to get emotional. He quietly explained, "About ten years ago, Uncle Charley brought me here and gave me specific instructions that if anything ever happened to him, I was to bring you here on this day. Your anniversary. He loved you so much, he worried about you being alone. But he told me he knew you were strong and would be okay."

They walked over to the bench that was placed at the top of a ridge overlooking the lake. Joe brushed off the bench and wrapped the blanket around his aunt before she sat down. Joe sat next to her in silence and they took in the tranquil beauty surrounding them. The water was frozen and covered in slick, shiny ice. The sun was glistening off the snow with such brightness that they could hardly open their eyes all the way. Trees along the water's edge were still covered with this morning's slight, wet snowfall. They could see their breath in the air but it felt refreshing, not cold. They sat in silence each in their own thoughts for quite some time. Ada broke the silence. "Thank you, Joey."

"It was my pleasure, Aunt A."

"Did he tell you about this place?" Ada asked.

"Not really. Just to bring you here on December 24th."

"This is the spot where he asked me to marry him. It seems like yesterday. We came back every year on our anniversary. Some years it was rather nasty weather but we did it anyway. It made it more of an adventure on those years. We came other times during the year too, but today was always the most special. The very first time we were here, he started making up this story about that spot in the water, right there." She pointed across the lake to an open spot where the ground sloped right to the water's edge. "He told me there was an underground town down there just waiting to be discovered. Its only light to the outside world was through a large underwater window. That's how they could tell the difference between day and night. Each year he would add characters to the story and tell adventures about their life down there. I always wondered if one year he would tell me that they had been rescued." She had a smile on her face as she reminisced about the stories.

Joe put his arm around her and studied her face for a few minutes. He said, "I think they were rescued. They are going to be just fine."

Ada nodded in satisfaction. "I think so, too."

THE END

Made in the USA
Monee, IL
27 September 2024